Copyright © 2001 by Lew Holton

Published in the United States by Beach Hooch Books.

Cover design by Tres Holton

# THE SEASON OF PREACHER JACK

## A Novel

by

## Lew Holton

BEACH HOOCH BOOKS  Murrells Inlet, SC

# CHAPTER ONE

*Summer 1961*

I was sitting on top of the cold drink box sipping a Nu-Grape soda and catching the fan breeze twice--once on its frontward and once on its backward sweep across the interior of the store--and Mr. Marion Graham was standing at the cash register when I asked Preacher Jack if he wasn't afraid of going to hell--the word "hell" kind of slipped out before I could catch it--like some folks were saying he was going to on account of his turning his back on the ministry--which according to what some people said was basically the same thing as turning your back on the Lord.

"Nope," he said, and then to Mr. Graham without missing a beat, "That'll be $1.19. I 'preciate it, and you come back real soon."

He said that last part to Mr. Graham's back, because Mr. Graham had kind of drawn up like he was trying to make himself as small a target as possible in case any lightning bolts came streaking through the roof and had started moving toward the door while he was still counting the correct change out in a trail across the counter, and then the screen door slapped shut behind him. Jack just picked up the change and asked me if I knew what *pre-cocious* meant. I told him I didn't reckon I did, and he said I might want to look it up sometime in the dictionary because I was likely to hear it again in the future.

"Though I have made my own genuine peace with the Christian belief system--" that's the way Preacher Jack's last Sunday morning speech to the congregation at our old church began--and my momma and my aunt and five or six other people said they'd never heard that particular way of putting it--Christian belief system, I mean--"I have become increasingly *un*peaceful with the way it is being preached and perpetuated by just about everybody, including myself."

I don't guess he could've stunned everybody any more if he'd've walked through the congregation and thwocked each one individually right square in the forehead with a ball-peen hammer. He'd tossed preachments from the pulpit before that had kerplunked into the calm world of certain people's thinking and had set murmurs rippling across the surface of the Sunday faces. But nothing like this. Rita Enslow said later that that's what we got for hiring a preacher who was a single man. If he'd've had a wife to keep him in line and maybe a couple of kids to think about, she told us, none of this would've ever happened. Some agreed with her; some didn't. I tend to think he'd been fighting it for some time. Something about the way everything was going along just like usual and then right in the middle of the last verse of "The Old Rugged Cross"--I say the last verse, but we don't ever do all of them; we always just do the first and last verses--anyway, he just stopped--waved his hands and shook his head and just stopped--and said, "Wait, wait. Listen--I'm sorry--but we have to talk." Something about the way it came on him like that--right in the middle of things--makes me think he'd been fighting it for a long time, and nothing in the world--not some perfect wife that Rita Enslow might've picked out for him or enough kids to put on a little theatre version of *The Sound of Music*--could've prevented it. Inevitable, I guess, is the word.

When he finished, he just walked up the aisle and out the door, and left everybody sitting there. No sermon. No hymn of invitation. No Doxology. Not even a last swipe of the collection plate.

"Preacher Jack," I said, then took a swig of grape soda, "I'm just not sure I understand exactly what it was you did that makes folks talk about you so much."

"Well," he said back, "I guess you could say I challenged them."

Preacher Jack had a way of talking to you and looking at you that made you feel like he was talking to you and looking at you just like he did with grown-ups. You knew he knew you were still a kid, but he had some kind of way of treating you like a kid when you were feeling like you needed to be a kid, and treating you like a real grown-up person at other times when a lot of people might've given you the ah-you're-just-a-kid-it's-none-of-your-business-yet treatment.

"Challenged 'em how?" I asked.

"Made 'em have to think, Slick," he replied. "Lot of people don't like that."

I held my bottle of grape soda up and took a reading on how much I had left and figured I was halfway through. "What'd you make 'em think about?"

"About Jesus," Preacher Jack said. "It's been my experience that people don't like to think too much about Jesus. Oh, they like to pray to Him and sing about Him."

"You mean like Him wantin' me for a sunbeam and all?" I asked.

"Yeah--like that. And some folks like to talk an awful lot about Him."

Preacher Jack walked over and got a box of toothpicks off one of the shelves, took a dime out of his pocket and crossed back to the cash register, rang up 10¢ and dropped the dime in the cash register drawer. Only then did he open the box, take out a toothpick and stick it in his mouth, and offer me one. I always thought it was funny that he paid himself for things he used in his own store. I took a toothpick.

"Thank you," I said.

"You're welcome," he said back. "But, with all that singing and praying and talking, most of 'em don't really want to do too much *thinking* about the ol' boy."

I believe I began to see right there part of the problem that people had with Preacher Jack. Or at least why they found him such a curiosity. I had never been president or vice-president or secretary-treasurer of the Sunday school class or anything like that, but even I knew that it was pretty high strange to refer to Jesus as "the ol' boy." And I said so, right out-loud.

"Strange is just strange, though," he said. "It's when we start equating strange with sinful that something ugly starts growing in people."

And that reminded me of something one of my uncles showed me one time, and I said, "Hey-- don't make me get ugly with you," and I hooked the tips of my thumbs in my nostrils and stretched them up and pulled down on my lower eyelids with my fingers at the same time and scrunched my mouth all crooked.

Preacher Jack said, "You know, Slick--if your face froze like that...it'd be a considerable improvement."

That's what I meant about Preacher Jack letting you have those "kid moments" when they came up. He could shift gears like that and never miss a beat.

While we were laughing, Delmer Tukes came in and just stood there looking at us, and I knew if there had been anybody else but Preacher Jack there, Delmer would've said flat-out what the expression on his face was saying. I could hear it in my mind just as clear as if he had said it, anyway-- "What're *you* laughin' at, ass-wipe?"

Delmer Tukes was the only boy any of us knew who qualified as what they referred to in the TV shows and the movies as a juvenile delinquent. At fifteen, he had already been sent to reform school twice. But the Tukes lived their lives like it made no difference--like reform school and jail were just other things you did. The only reason Delmer was back home now was that his mother-- whose face always looked to me like the face of that Indian on a buffalo nickel, except made out of leather--had gone to the authorities and told a bald-faced lie that she had a heart condition and needed Delmer at home to help look after her. Misruss

Tukes--I never knew her first name and if any of the adults knew it, they never said it--they just called her Misruss Tukes, too--cut yards all over the neighborhood. That's what she did for a living. In the summertime, you'd hear her lawnmower crank up right after the sun came up on Saturday mornings, and when you looked, there she'd be--hunched over the mower, a wide-brimmed straw hat shading her face, wearing the same blue-jean overalls she always wore, shearing stripe after stripe of that shaggy fescue and rye and wild onion and Johnson grass jungle that passed for lawns in our neighborhood, all the time with that expression on her face like the grass had done something to offend her personally and now it was pay-back time. She had a heart condition like I had a love life.

"My momma sent me for two packs of them Pall Malls," Delmer said.

He wasn't fooling anybody.

"Why, I don't believe I've ever seen your momma smoke," Preacher Jack replied.

"I don't believe you ever seen 'er shit neither, preacher," Delmer said back, never blinking. "There's just some things she b'lieves a lady don't do in public."

Preacher Jack set two packs of smokes on the counter.

"You tell her I'm praying for her--that those

cigarettes don't aggravate that heart condition of hers," he said, and he didn't blink either. "That'll be 42¢."

Delmer took a handful of change out of his pocket and slowly and deliberately snapped four dimes and two pennies onto the counter.

"I'll tell her, preacher," he said--then picked up the cigarettes and pushed the screen door open with his foot, "but I 'xpect she'll be just fine without your prayers."

The screen door slammed behind him, then we heard him hawk and spit, and we both knew Preacher Jack was going to have to clean something real nasty off one of the gas pumps.

I knew, though, that he wouldn't say anything to Delmer--not that Jack was the least bit intimidated by him. In fact, he was one of the few people who absolutely stood his ground in Delmer's presence--not in a confrontational way, just sort of the way an old oak tree stands its ground. Almost everybody else, grown-ups included, cut a wide swath around Delmer. Though Delmer was big for his age, it wasn't so much his size as his menacing demeanor that folks avoided.

Delmer was missing his right index finger. The only other person I knew who had lost a finger was my cousin Danny, who was bitten on the little finger of his right hand by a copperhead. Being the only person most people knew who had actually been snake-bit, too, Danny was something of a celebrity. Until then, it was commonly accepted among everyone I knew that if you got bitten by a poisonous snake, you just died a terrible, agonizing death.

Every summer someone would tell the story of some guy who had gone swimming in a creek and thought he'd gotten tangled up in submerged barbed wire, only to discover to his horror that he had blundered into the proverbial "nest of water moccasins." It was a wonderful tale of serpentine terror.

One of the local deputy sheriffs, Don Lightsey, also told a story of the time he went on a raid of a moonshine still in the woods, and while creeping up on the operation, he stepped on a rattlesnake. He realized that the snake was pinned to the ground by his boot--the snake's head barely extending beyond the edge of his bootsole. He knew he couldn't shoot the snake without alerting the moonshiners, who would start shooting back, and he couldn't lift his foot without having the snake turn and bite him. So, he said, he took out his hunting knife and quietly sawed the snake's head off. He liked to show the souvenir--sixteen rattles and a button--to cap off the story.

Danny's encounter was almost boring by

comparison. He had been mowing the grass near a storage building at the back of his family's lot in the country. Several bamboo fishing poles lay on the ground next to the old building, and when Danny picked them up to move them so that he could mow there, three small copperheads were lying on top of the poles. They slid down the poles as he raised them, and one of the snakes bit him on the little finger. The loss of the finger was more the result of an improper tourniquet and bungled first-aid than actual snake bite damage, but still it was a legitimate snake bite, and the story had just enough of the "nest of snakes" element to bathe Danny in the aura of miraculous survivor celebrity. He was just lucky, everybody agreed, that they hadn't been rattlesnakes or moccasins.

There were two stories about how Delmer came to lose the finger. One story was that he had gotten into a fight with a Cherokee Indian kid during one of his stays at reform school. Supposedly, Delmer tried to cut the braid that the Indian kid wore in his hair. In the course of the fight, the Cherokee kid had bitten Delmer's finger off. According to the story, the Indian wore the finger bone on a string around his neck. The other story was that Delmer's older brother, Doyle, had been in the Army very briefly, but had gotten a Bad Conduct Discharge because of all the trouble he caused. The story was that Doyle hated the Army so much that, when he got home, he held Delmer down and shot Delmer's trigger finger off with a pistol to keep the Army from ever getting Delmer. I didn't know anybody who had ever asked Delmer which story was true.

I knew that if it ever came down to it, Delmer would simply pulverize me. Not only was I younger, but I was small for my age--not to mention that my scrapping abilities were largely untested.

The one fight I had been in had happened at the beginning of the last school year. Vern Kennedy had experienced what people called a growth spurt during the previous summer, and when he showed up for the start of the fifth grade, he found himself a full head taller than most of the others. And something in the new mix of hormones and altitude had also activated his bully gene, it seemed.

I never figured out exactly what I had done-- I suspect I had done nothing more than be infuriatingly small and pickuponable--but at lunch one Friday Vern announced to me and all others within earshot that after school he was going to kick my butt. He punctuated the announcement with a stiff-fingered poke to my chest. It all came as quite a surprise to me, but I did my best to take the news with what gumption I could muster.

Nonetheless, after school I didn't waste any

time looking for Vern; I hopped on my bike and started for home. I had barely made it to the edge of the schoolyard when I heard him holler at me. I looked back and saw Vern mounting his own bicycle and starting after me. I considered trying to outrun him, but there were enough kids watching that the embarrassment factor kicked in, and though I didn't speed up, I continued my steady pedaling. Vern sped up along side of me just as we got to the first house past the school, reached out and pushed me, and I veered into the front yard of the house. I lay my bike down and stood there. Vern dropped his bike, stalked up to me, and shoved me.

In the background, I could see a number of kids from school who had gathered to watch. Mostly Vern seemed to be a pusher and a shover, throwing his new height and weight around, but then he punched me in the chest, and I went down into the grass. I landed beside a rubber garden hose that lay in loose coils on the lawn. As Vern turned to sneer and laugh at the kids who had gathered behind him at the edge of the yard, I seized the hose about four feet from the end. Though I knew it probably wasn't absolutely fair in the bare-handed fighting sense, neither did the bulk behind Vern's bare hands seem terribly fair at the moment.

I swung the hose, bola fashion, in one swooping revolution above my head, and just as

Vern turned back to me, I caught him with the threaded brass end of the hose just below his left eye. He howled and grabbed at his face. For one terrifying instant I was afraid I had put his eye out, but when he lowered his hands to look at the blood on them, I could see his eye was okay. He ran back towards the school. The other kids just stood and gaped.

I dropped the hose and stood there, as well--waiting I suppose for the full wrath of teachers, the principal, parents, police, and whatever other adults might want to get in on the action to come for me. But no one came. After what seemed like a long time, the other kids began to leave, so I picked up my bike, got on, and headed home.

When I got there, I told my mother only that this bully--Vern Kennedy--had come after me after school and that we had gotten in a fight. She asked if I was okay, and I said, "Yes, ma'am," and she asked if he was okay, and I said, "Yes, ma'am, I think so." And she said I'd have to tell my dad when he got home, and that was it.

My dad was not what you would call a talker. When I told him, he just nodded, then he asked me what happened. I told him--about the kids watching and about the garden hose. He just nodded again.

After a few moments of silence, he said, "I

had a big guy come after me one time."

"What happened?" I asked.

"He sucker-punched me," he said, but he wasn't looking right at me. Instead he was looking somewhere...away...like he was remembering.

"Oh," I said, though I wasn't sure exactly what a sucker-punch was. I pictured something involving a toilet plunger, though I knew that was too cartoonish to be anything like what he was talking about. "What happened then?"

"I got him around the neck," my father demonstrated on an imaginary opponent--locking his right arm around the big guy's imaginary neck. He grabbed his right wrist with his left hand, creating what looked like a headlock configuration. "Then I just held on and squeezed," he said.

"Did it work?" I asked.

"Flung me around like a rag doll," my dad said, "but eventually, yeah, it worked. Almost choked him to death."

I couldn't really picture my dad choking anybody nearly to death, so it was my turn to just nod.

"You probably won't have any more problems out of him," he said.

"I hope not," I answered.

Vern showed up at school on Monday with a bandage on his cheek, and he glared at me, but--my dad was right--he didn't pick on anybody for the rest of the school year. Still--Vern Kennedy, I knew, was no Delmer Tukes.

"You know," said Preacher Jack, "for a large part of my life, I have truly believed that there wasn't a soul on earth who wasn't one well-timed hymn away from salvation. But..." he took the toothpick out of the corner of his mouth and started for the door, "...I don't know if there's enough praying and preaching and bring-tears-to-your-eyes singing at the whole Southern Baptist Seminary to do that Tukes boy any good."

"He's a mean 'un," I allowed.

Preacher Jack went out to clean the gas pump, and I turned up the bottle of grape soda and polished it off and froze to see if there was a big grape burp in the deal, but there didn't seem to be, so I hopped down from the drink box and went and put the bottle in the wooden crate with the other empties.

## Chapter Two

I had been into the store probably a dozen times before Jack pointed to my navy blue baseball cap with the New York logo and commented, "You a Yankees fan?"

I was a Yankees convert. Though it somehow seemed disloyal to my Southern upbringing to take up the banner of a team with such a disdainful moniker, the lure of the diamond heroics of the Bronx Bombers had proven irresistible--Whitey Ford, Yogi Berra, Bobby Richardson, Clete Boyer, and, of course, the Mick. How could you *not* be a Mickey Mantle fan? Without a local major league team around to root for, a kid's allegiance was fairly easy pickings for the likes of the Yankees.

My friend Gilbert's grandmother had been an unlikely influence, as well. Originally from Brooklyn, Granny Sligh, as she was known to almost everyone, lived with Gilbert and his parents. Like any true Brooklynite, Granny Sligh had been a die-hard Brooklyn Dodgers fan, but then they committed the unpardonable--they moved to Los Angeles. The act was heresy of biblical proportions. She used to say that God may forgive Walter O'Malley and the Bums, but she never would. The Giants had made a move, as well—to San

Francisco—and I'm not sure if Granny Sligh's Yankee fervor was the result of a process of elimination--a winnowing down of her choices of New York baseball teams--or just orneriness-- Yankee fan-dom to spite the Dodgers--but she saw to it that every televised Yankees game shimmered alluringly across the TV screen at the Campbell's house, and Gilbert and I were right there to take the pin-striped bait. I spent an awful lot of time at Gilbert's house. It was safe to say I was a Yankees fan.

"Yessir," I answered Jack.

"Me, too," he said. "See that game yesterday? Roger Maris hit two home runs."

I reached up and tugged on the bill of my cap and looked up at Jack. "Mantle hit one, too," I pointed out, as if I needed to defend the Mick.

Jack was tall. I say that as objectively as possible for someone still shy of twelve years of age and closer to the four foot mark than the five foot one. In fact, I wouldn't hit five feet until well into high school, though that's one of those things I was probably better off not knowing at the time. Even taking all that into consideration, though, Jack was tall.

At some point later in the summer, Jack would tell me about the first Sunday that he had preached at our church. After the service, he said, he was shaking hands with folks at the door as they left, and as he took Rita Enslow's hand and said to her, "Thank you for being here this morning," she had looked up at him and said, "You're...*tall*."

"Yes, ma'am," he'd said, "I have been blessed with a fairly lofty view of the world."

And still gazing up at him, Rita Enslow had said, "You must really have to trim your nose hair a lot."

"Yes, ma'am," Jack said he answered again, "it's the very condition for which the term 'a constant battle' was coined."

I didn't doubt him. It sounded just like something Rita Enslow would say.

Looking up at him now, though, I wasn't thinking about nose hair.

"Good game," Jack said, "'course the Angels aren't much of a threat. We'll have to see how they do against the Indians."

"Yessir," I said to Jack, but to myself I said, "Mantle ain't scared of no Indians."

Preachers come and go, I guess, for all kinds of reasons, but it was the manner of his leaving-- that and the fact that he only went down the road a short piece--that made Jack Blair *the* topic of conversation in Pineville the rest of the summer of 1961. Lots of folks referred to his place as the

Pump-n-Preach--and said it in that kind of sniffy-laugh-through-your-nose way that means "yeah, I'm just waitin' to laugh when you slip and fall on your ass"--but neither the dish towels that the Shell station gave with a fill-up, nor the red and blue and green and yellow striped drinking glasses that the Pure station gave out could compete with the tug at folks' curiosity when Jack opened Blair's Little Store and Gas Station. And a lot of his former parishioners decided it couldn't hurt to pull in for just a dollar's worth of Regular. Being a kid at the time, I didn't really need an excuse to go by. I didn't know any better. Everybody said so.

# CHAPTER THREE

"Slick?" Preacher Jack called from outside.

By the way, the nickname doesn't *mean*
anything. I asked my momma once why everybody
called me Slick, and she said, "Your daddy just
started calling you that when you were real little,
and so everybody else did, too." That wasn't
exactly what I was hoping for. I knew it wasn't
something dramatic like, "When you were little,
you fell down an oil well, and when they rescued
you, you were covered in slick black Texas crude."
But I thought there might be *something* to it--
something more than "your daddy just started
calling you that." Some people have real names
with nicknames practically built-in, like William
turns right into Bill, or Robert to Bobby. Even if
you're stuck with a really awful real name like
Buchanan or something, Buchanan turns into
Bucky--at least it did for one of the kids in my class
last year. Some of us, though, just have names that
don't turn into anything. They're just what they
are. So, if you get a nickname, it's Bubba or Sport
or Ace...or Slick. Nicknames that don't *mean*
anything.

I went to the door and hollered back through
the screen, "Sir?"

"Your daddy just turned in your driveway,"

he said. "Were you supposed to get anything for your momma while you were here?" he asked.

"No, sir."

"Well...I reckon I'll see you tomorrow then."

"Yessir; I reckon so."

And it seems I had succeeded in wasting another summer day of my childhood exactly as childhood summer days were intended to be wasted. Mission accomplished, I headed for home and, being a Friday evening, if I was lucky, hamburgers on the outdoor grill.

'Course my nickname, you'll notice, wasn't Lucky. I suppose that the taste of liver is something that's acquired. I always likened the taste to holding a penny on your tongue while you were eating clay-dirt--not that I'd ever done those things, but those were the images that the taste conjured in my mouth. At least these were chicken livers--one of my dad's favorites--rather than the big slabs of beef liver. I got to be pretty good at palming a chicken liver and slipping it into my pocket to be disposed of outside later. But it just wasn't humanly possible to palm them all. A couple of them were bound to end up in your mouth, and all I can say is thank God for white bread and mashed potatoes--while they couldn't kill the taste, they did manage to alter the texture just enough so that a guy could get a few bites of the nasty brown organ down.

After supper and after we'd cleared the table and washed the dishes, my mom went to the bottom drawer of the sideboard and took out the lace tablecloth, and I knew company was coming over.

"Are the Campbells coming over to play cards tonight?" I asked.

"Yes," my mother said, "but it's only canasta."

The last part was for the benefit of whoever keeps track of every single thing we say and do in life and why we say and do it. Apparently, playing cards was *usually* a sin, because, I reasoned, it meant playing card games with sinful sounding names, like stud poker and blackjack and gin rummy, so you had to be sure to distinguish out-loud that you were only playing *canasta*, which was, I supposed, one of the allowable exceptions to the sinning that usually accompanied card-playing.

"Is Gilbert coming?" I asked.

"Well, I'm sure he is," she answered.

"I'll be outside, if it's okay," I said.

"Where're you going?" Momma asked.

"Just to the street light," I told her.

"All right," she said, "but don't go past the street light."

"I won't," I said, and I was out the back

door.

There was a time when I would've waited around for the Campbells to get there and to see if Gilbert wanted to come outside and goof around while the grown-ups played cards--canasta, I mean--but since Gilbert had turned 13 and was going to be going to junior high school this year, he'd changed. Even though I was only a little more than a year younger--well, either you were going to junior high school or you weren't. If you were, you weren't necessarily a grown-up or anything, but if you weren't, you surely were still just a kid. And most people who had just achieved that mysterious no-longer-a-kid stage didn't want to hang out with those who were identifiably still just kids. So I felt no obligation to hang around and see if Gilbert wanted to join me. If he wanted to, he would. If he didn't, he wouldn't. It was his call.

I picked up an old ping-pong paddle from off the back porch and headed for the street light, trying to think of something really good to do with the four chicken livers in my pocket.

I put one of the chicken livers out in the middle of the street in what would be the far shallows of the pool of street light illumination. I'm not sure what I thought might be attracted to the chicken liver, or what I thought I might do when whatever it was that might *be* attracted to it went for the chicken liver bait, so mainly I just squatted there in the shadowy part of the dark and waited. Off in the distance, I could see the light on down at the Little Store.

On the road where my house was, about two hundred yards down, on the other side of the street, stood an historical marker. "The Sutton House. On February 12, 1865 Jefferson Davis spent the night here on his way to the last meeting of the Cabinet of the Confederate States of America." A brick chimney and a couple of steps leading to nowhere were all that remained of the old house. My friends and I decided that Sherman had burned the place--in retaliation for the Suttons having provided a bed to Jefferson Davis. We used to search the grounds for minie balls embedded in old trees or the buried bones of long-dead Yankees. Once, we found some bones, but they turned out to belong to a mule. In truth, the old place more likely fell to termites and kudzu.

Just past the marker, several years before I was born, Mr. Clarence Brown built a gas station and little store. The Little Store must have been easy to name. If it had been a house, it would have been what you might call a cottage. You could have fit one bedroom and one other room--a living room and kitchenette combination, maybe--inside the structure. It was a white clapboard building with heaven-only-knows how many coats of paint--the cracks and blisters of each undercoat fighting its way back to the surface. The only windows were the two on the front, one on either side of the door. There was a screen door, a bit pot-bellied, with a sturdy spring that, given the opportunity, yanked it closed with a fine, square slap, and there was the wooden door, which had once been green and probably still was beneath the tin signs that now armored most of it--one RC Cola sign; a Tube Rose Snuff sign; and one that featured Martha White Flour, Plain or Self-Rising. There were bars on the windows, which rendered them almost impossible to clean. The green tin roof was steeply pitched. There was no sign with the store hours posted--there was no need--you just looked to see if Jack's Volkswagen was parked beside the building. If it was there, the store was open. Preacher Jack was the only person I knew who drove one of the Bugs-- I mean, I'd certainly seen others, but I didn't actually know the people who drove them. Jack's Bug was a faded-looking light-green late 1950s model--the exact year didn't seem to be important. Out front of the store, the two gas pumps and the air pump at the service island were covered with a white frame tin-roofed shelter. The parking lot was unpaved, but there were enough rocks and gravel so that the lot wasn't reduced to pure mud when it rained. On dry days, every car stirred a small cloud of fine, gray, powdery dust that settled itself on the impossible to clean windows and the pumps. A simple keyless light fixture over the door, into which was screwed a single yellow bug-light, struggled to cast its jaundiced pool of light all the way out to the pumps after the sun went down.

While I was squatting there on the side of the road, I picked up one of the remaining livers, tossed it up, and swatted it with the ping-pong paddle. I peered into the dark and listened--for what, I'm not sure--and when I looked back toward the street, I could just barely make out the face of a yellow dog at the edge of the darkness. I knew he had to be a stray because of the way he hung back-- his fear of people playing tug of war with his hunger for the chicken liver. For a second I had a twinge of "uh oh," wondering if he might be rabid or something, but then I realized that if he was rabid, he wouldn't be hanging back like he was, so-- real softly--I started talking to the creature.

"You hungry, boy? ... Are you? ... It's okay, boy; ain't nobody gonna hurt you. ... You know, I used to have a dog and he loved them things. ... I don't have much use for 'em myself, but don't tell my momma. ... It's okay; go ahead. ... I got some more, you know, if you like that one."

The dog had inched forward a bit, trying to

watch me and the chicken liver at the same time.

"That's a good boy. ... You eat that one, and I'll give you another one. ... You look like you hadn't had much to eat. You a stray, boy? ... Don't be scared."

Slowly the dog moved forward, his nostrils opening and closing, collecting the scent of the liver and me both. He stretched his head forward, froze for a second, then picked up the piece of liver with his mouth, almost daintily.

"There you go, boy. Zat good stuff?"

With a quick motion, he snapped his jaws slightly forward and wolfed the chicken liver down.

"Don't think you even had a chance to taste that, did you, boy? ... Want another one?"

I held another of the livers in my hand and slowly stretched it forward. The yellow dog backed off, almost back into the shadows but not quite. His nostrils worked again. Slowly I lowered my hand, and with as soft an underhanded toss as I could manage, I arched the chicken liver toward the animal. He skittered back into the dark and stood sideways, looking at me, trying to figure out if I'd assaulted him or fed him, ready to flee if he sensed the slightest threat.

"It's just some more liver, boy. It's okay."

The chicken liver had landed nearer the center of the pool of light. He would have to venture closer if he wanted the second treat. He took a tentative step and then another toward the liver, paused, and looked at me.

I squatted there and stayed as still as a statue, and just when I was starting to play with the idea in my head that there didn't seem to be any statues of anybody squatting that I ever saw or heard of, a mosquito landed on my cheek. I knew if I swatted it, the yellow dog would be gone. I knew, too, what was going to happen if I didn't swat it. Too late--I felt it stab my cheek, and the sweat broke out on my forehead.

I remembered hearing one of my uncles who had been in the Marines and who had been on Guadalcanal talking about lying in the jungle one night and hearing the Japs and feeling the mosquitoes biting and knowing that, if he slapped at the mosquito that was drilling away at his neck, the Japs'd hear and would open up on him and his buddies, and so he just lay there and let that mosquito drink its fill. And so I froze there and thought to myself that this was good practice for if I ever found myself in a similar combat situation, and then I thought--yeah, but I bet if I move my hand verrrrry slowly, I can flick that sucker away without making any noise or any sudden movement--and so I eased my hand up toward my cheek, figuring I might even be able to squash it between my thumb and forefinger. But just as my hand touched my own cheek, of course, I felt it lift off and heard it buzz by my ear as it flew off. I pictured it heavy with a bellyful of my blood.

"I ain't gonna hurt you, boy. Shoot--I want you to have it. Better you than me."

I scratched my cheek and glanced up the street, afraid that after all I'd gone through with the mosquito a car might come down the street and scare Ol' Yeller, as I was starting to think of the dog. But the street was quiet. The dog crept forward a bit more--almost to the liver now.

"There you go, boy. Git it. ... I got one more if you want it."

He lowered his head toward the liver, still keeping his eyes on me, and grabbed the morsel. He seemed to get two chews on that one.

"Pretty good stuff, huh? You want the other one? Do you, boy? ... Alright. ... I'm gonna hafta toss it, so don't be scared again, okay? ... Okay, here it comes, boy."

Again, I tossed the liver in a small arc toward the dog. And, again, he backed up, though this time not all the way back into the shadows. The liver landed about halfway between where I was and where the last piece had been. I realized I was luring him closer to me. He seemed to realize it, too. Neither one of us knew why.

"That's a good boy. ... Come on and get it; it's all right."

I wished I hadn't wasted the first liver, swatting it away with the ping-pong paddle. I wondered if I'd kept it if I could get him to eat it out of my hand--wondered which one of us would chicken out if it came down to that. He had come forward in small steps, one or two at a time, almost to the third treat. He lowered his head, extended his neck, reached for it, and--smack!--the rock ricocheted off the pavement right by his head. It smacked so hard it flashed sparks, and the dog yelped and bolted into the darkness, and I jumped and made some startled sound of my own, and Gilbert's harsh laugh leaped out of the dark, all at the same time.

"Damn it, Gilbert! You scared the shit out of me!"

"That's a good puppy-wuppy," Gilbert mocked in a kind of girlish falsetto, then laughed again. "What a dip-wad! You shoulda seen y'all jump. What a wuss! Did you think some werewolf or something out of the dark had you?"

"'S not funny, Gilbert. 'S not funny a damn bit."

"Looked pretty funny from where I was standin'. Besides--I probably saved your life, you know."

"What're you talkin' about? Saved my life, my butt."

"Yeah, your life and your butt, too. That was a stray, ya know--probably one of them wild dogs."

"Yeah. So what?"

"They hunt in packs, ya know. They get one of the shaky-lookin' ones like that to get your attention, get you to get all crouched down and talkin' baby talk--he made a kind of kissing sound with his lips--'Come 'ere, boy; come on'--and meanwhile the rest of the pack are sneakin' up on you in the dark. I heard some guy in the barber shop say they got 'em a little girl last year over the other side of the county--killed her and half ate her before somebody scared 'em off."

"Huh uh."

"Uh huh."

"You're full of it."

"Oh, yeah? Well, if they'd've come pouncin' in here out of the dark, I got something for 'em."

"Whadda you mean you got something for 'em?"

"Just what I said. I got something for 'em. And I don't mean chicken livers."

"What is it?"

For a moment I wondered if he'd gotten one of those high-powered slingshots that shot ball-bearings. I'd seen one down at the hardware store the last time I went there with my dad. He was getting the lawnmower blade sharpened, and while we waited I wandered around the store and made a mental list of everything I'd buy if I had a million dollars, and I was up to two hundred and eighty-some-odd dollars worth of stuff when I'd seen the slingshot. It was packaged with a bag of steel ball-bearings and a cardboard target that showed a bobcat with target rings drawn on it, and while I was thinking about how you'd only get one chance to nail a bobcat with a ball-bearing before he either ran off or sprang right on you, my dad put his hand on my shoulder and I jumped and he asked what I was so jumpy about and I just said, "nothing"--that I was just thinking and hadn't heard him walk up, and he said the lawnmower blade was ready, and we left. I never did finish spending the million dollars.

"Swear you won't tell nobody?" asked Gilbert.

"I won't tell. What is it, a slingshot?"

"Slingshots are for kids and wusses," he said.

I started to say something about that, but I saw that it would only lead to a no-win situation for me if I did, so I just said again, "I won't tell nobody."

"Swear," he said.

"I swear."

"Swear to God and say you hope your mom gets brain cancer if you ever tell."

"I'm not gonna say that about my mother!"

"What're you--scared?"

"No. I'm just not gonna say that about my mother."

"All right. Swear to God, then, and say you hope you go blind and get polio both if you ever tell."

"Jeez, Gilbert--what the hell is it?" I said, unable to imagine what might need the double guarantee of blindness *and* polio to safeguard its secrecy.

"Say it or I'm not showin' you."

"Okay," I said, "I swear to God I won't tell nobody and hope to go blind and get polio if I'm lyin'."

"All right then," he said, and he sat down and pulled up his pants leg and reached into the top of his boot.

I watched his hand very gingerly pull out what looked like a real pistol.

"Holy shit, Gilbert," I said. "That looks like--I mean, is that real?"

"Colt .25 automatic," he said. "My dad keeps it in his tackle box."

"What are you doin' with it? He know you

have it?"

"'Course he don't know I got, dipstick. I snuck it out and was gonna go out in the woods and try it out when my mom and dad called me and told me to come on 'cause we were comin' over here."

"You were gonna shoot it?"

"No--I was gonna throw it up in the air and see if it would fly. 'Course I was gonna shoot it. I've shot my dad's .22 plenty of times."

"Yeah, but that's a rifle."

"Yeah, well, so?"

"So it's just different, is all."

"You are such a wuss; you know that? Anyway, looks like I'll have to sneak it back into the tackle box when we get home and wait 'til I get another chance to go try it out."

"Jeez, Gilbert, I don't know."

"Yeah, well, if that pack of wild dogs had come out of the dark after you, I bet you'd know. You just remember to keep your mouth shut about it. Blind and polio-crippled, remember?"

"Yeah, I remember."

"Good. You just keep rememberin'." He put the gun back into his boot. "I'm goin' back to the house."

"Yeah, me, too," I said, and watched him stand up and adjust his pants leg over the top of his boot.

We walked back toward my house--Gilbert listening for wild dogs in the darkness and me inexplicably more scared of the secret I knew was in Gilbert's boot than anything I thought might be lurking out there in the dark.

# Chapter Four

Jack was sweeping the store's worn wooden floor, but he stopped when I came in.

"Mornin', Slick," he said.

"Mornin'."

"Whatcha got planned for the 4th tomorrow?"

"There's picnic at the church, but I don't know if we're going." I looked around the store.

"Hotdogs and softball?" Preacher Jack asked.

"Yessir," I said. "We went to church yesterday. They had a visiting preacher."

"That's good."

"Miss Lillian Breckenridge sang a solo. She sang real high and did that thing with her voice like she's trying to sound like an opera singer." I looked around some more.

"Well, Miss Lillian's real proud of her voice," Jack said.

"The preacher sang a solo, too," I said. "How come you never sang a solo when you were the preacher?"

"Mostly because I sing real bad, Slick."

"Oh," I said. It was easy to say something back to someone who did something well, but I wasn't sure what to say to someone who did

40

something badly. "*Real* bad?" is what came out.

"Pretty darn bad," Jack nodded his head.

"Oh," I said again, still searching for just the right thing to say back.

I thought of my Great-aunt Rose, who everybody knew sang really badly, and about whom they would talk and even laugh--only when she wasn't around to hear--because nobody wanted to tell her she sang really badly. I started to say something one time when I was much younger, but my mother pinched the back of my upper arm, and I interrupted myself with a really loud "Ow!" after which my mother took me off to my room to "change clothes," and told me if I couldn't say something nice about someone I shouldn't say anything at all. I could never think of anything nice to say about Aunt Rose's bad singing. I wasn't having any better luck coming up with something to say about Jack's. But I was curious about one thing.

"Did somebody *tell* you you sang real bad?" I asked.

"When I first went to the seminary," Jack said, "I didn't know yet that I sang quite so bad as I actually did. I sang enthusiastically, you might say. I guess I thought it was the same thing as good. I decided to try out for the choir, and so I did. I went and sang a very enthusiastic rendition of 'There Is a Fountain.' We had a Minister of Music there named

K.C. Welborne, who had this wonderful booming bass voice that could make the molecules of your soul vibrate when he hit certain notes. Boy, I wanted to be able to do that! But...after I'd finished singing, he said to me, 'Jack--you know--God can hear you singing in your heart. And for some people...well...that's enough. They don't really need to sing out loud.' I said, 'Are you saying I don't sing very well?' and K.C. said, 'I'm just saying that God can hear you just fine singing in your heart. And if that's good enough for Him, well, it's probably good enough for the rest of us, too.'"

"Were you mad?" I asked.

"No," said Jack, "not mad, really. I guess I was a little disappointed at first. But after a while I noticed that, when I sang real soft with my voice, I could hear myself singing in my heart, and I'll be darned if I didn't sound just like K.C."

We stood there without saying anything for a few seconds. Then--"I think I must do math pretty good in my heart," I said.

Jack laughed. "Did you come in for something in particular?" he asked.

"Oh, yessir--my momma sent me to see if you had any Pepto-Bismol and Sal Hepatica," I answered.

"I don't believe you're supposed to take both of those at the same time, Slick."

"Why not?" I asked.

"Well...they're for different problems." he said. "You sure she wanted both of them?"

"That's what she said."

Jack handed me the broom. "Here you go," he said, "Don't try to operate that. It's pulling a little to the left and might get away from you. I'll get the stuff for you."

I was real tempted to give the broom a try, but I fought the urge. Jack went back to one of the shelves at the rear of the store--a shelf stocked with aspirins and Goody's headache powders and mercurochrome and Bromo Seltzer and other tinctures and remedies.

"Hey," Jack called from the rear, "two more for Maris yesterday. And, yeah, yeah, I know-- Mantle got one, too. You know," he continued, as he came back with two bottles, "that puts Maris halfway to the record." He crossed to the counter and put the bottles in a small brown bag.

"Mantle has 28," I piped up, as I handed him the two dollars my mother had given me.

"Who knows," Jack said, and he rang up the purchase, "Ruth better watch out. This may be the year one of them catches him." He handed me back the change.

As I stuffed the coins into the pocket of my jeans, I said, "I don't know..." with what I thought was a fair approximation of the skepticism I'd heard the TV sports announcers voice.

"Guess we'll just have to wait and see," Jack said, and he came around the counter and took back the broom. "You tell your mom I said 'hi' and I hope she feels better."

"Yessir," I said, "I will."

As I started out the door, Jack began to sweep again, then grabbed the broom as if it had veered off to the left suddenly and almost gotten away from him. "Whoa!" he said, "gonna have to work on the alignment on this thing."

# Chapter Five

I was sitting on some empty crates that were stacked up on the shady side of the store, when Preacher Jack came out to take the readings off his gas pumps and saw me.

"Whatcha doin'?" he asked.

"Nothin'," I answered. "Just thinkin'."

"Oh," he said. "Well, you got a good shady place for it."

"Yessir."

Jack walked over and began to record the numbers off the gas pumps onto the clipboard he was carrying--first the Regular pump, then the Hi-Test.

"My car's running a little ragged," he said. "You ever do a tune-up?"

"No, sir," I shook my head.

"Invaluable skill, Slick," Jack said, as he laid the clipboard on top of the old Volkswagen. "Otherwise, you're just at the mercy of luck and mechanics."

I nodded, as if I understood. Jack opened the trunk at the front of the car and reached inside and took out a toolbox and a lug wrench.

"How 'bout open her up in back," he said to me, and I went to rear of the car and opened the hood and looked down at the small engine. Jack set the toolbox down at the back of the car and pointed at the large pulley around which ran the fan belt. "See that spot of white paint?" he asked. I looked at the pulley and noted a small white line that looked as if it had been painted there with a fine-pointed brush. It was at approximately the eight o'clock position on the face of the wheel.

"Yessir," I said.

He handed me the lug wrench. "Do me a favor, if you will," he said. "Fit that lug wrench on the head of that big nut right in the middle of the pulley, and ease it around 'til that white line is right at the top of the wheel. While you're doing that, I'll get my tools out."

"Okay," I said and took the wrench. Jack opened his toolbox and began to rummage for the tools he wanted, and I slipped the socket of the wrench onto the head of the nut.

"Clockwise," Jack offered. I pushed down on the long handle of the lug wrench and felt the engine's resistance begin to give, as the white line eased upward toward the twelve o'clock position. When it got to the top, I stopped. Jack looked over, with a screwdriver and a couple of other things in his hands.

"Perfect," he said. "They call that top dead center." I nodded again. He set the tools down on a cloth at the rear of the vehicle. "You know what the distributor is?" he asked.

"I'm not sure," I replied.

"That humpy plastic-looking thing there with all the wires coming out of it."

"Oh, yeah," I said.

"It has two metal clips on the sides," he said. "See 'em?" Again, I nodded. "You might want to use the screwdriver to help you, but see if you can pop those clips loose for me while I get the parts I need out of the front."

Jack walked around to the front of the car, and I picked up the screwdriver. I couldn't believe he was letting me mess with the engine of his car. What if I broke something? Carefully, I inserted the tip of the screwdriver between one of the metal clips and the side of the distributor.

"Don't be afraid of it," Jack spoke from beneath the trunk lid in front. "You can't hurt anything."

I pried, and the clip popped loose. "Once you get the first one off, the other one usually comes right off," he said. I tried it. He was right. Jack came back with a couple of small yellow and red boxes in his hand. He looked at the distributor cap. "Good," he said. "Now let me show you what goes on inside."

He knelt down and pulled the distributor cap off to one side where it dangled by its wires. "I bought this car from a guy named Frankie," he said. "Knew him since we were kids together."

"I like it," I said.

"I like it, too," Jack said, "and so did Frankie at first." He took the screwdriver from me and pointed to a small mechanical contraption inside the distributor. "Those are the points," he said. "I think they need changing. We'll check." As he used the screwdriver to loosen the screw that held the points down, he continued, "Frankie was what you might call frugal. That's why he bought the car."

"Frugal?" I questioned.

"Some folks might say cheap. I prefer frugal."

"Ah." I understood.

"Frankie had heard that these little cars got great gas mileage. Which meant he'd have to buy less gas. Which would save him money." Jack removed the points and held the little spring-loaded mechanism out for me to see. He pulled back on the little metal arm. "See the ends there, Slick?" he asked, "those little hard pads--how they're kind of burnt and pitted-looking?" I looked and, indeed, could see what he meant. "We could file them," he said, "but...let's just go ahead and replace them."

"Okay," I agreed. Just like I had the final say-so on the matter.

Jack set the old points aside. "Frankie had a bad habit of bragging, too. He bragged and bragged about how much money this car was going to save him on gas, and after a few days of listening to him, some of his buddies got tired of hearing about it and decided to teach him a little lesson."

"What kind of lesson?" I asked.

"Well, they set up a schedule, and every night for two weeks, one of the guys would sneak over to Frankie's house with a gas can and fill the car's gas tank." Jack removed a small metal cylinder with a wire attached to it from inside the distributor. "This is the condenser," he said. "It's probably okay, but if you're changing the points, it just makes sense to go ahead and put a new condenser in while you're at it."

I nodded, as if to say, "Sure. Everybody knows that."

"Naturally, over the course of the couple of weeks," Jack went on, "Frankie's stories about the car's incredible economy and performance grew to legendary proportions. Then...his buddies changed tactics." Jack opened the two little boxes and took out the new points and condenser.

"What'd they do?"

"Each night for the next two weeks, one of them would siphon off about half the tank." Jack smiled. "At first, the guy was just real quiet. Then he became sullen."

"Sullen?"

"Like pouting."

"Ah." That I understood.

"He took the car to the shop. He had tune-ups done. He started cussing what he called 'those stupid Krauts' and their idiot ideas about automotive engineering." Jack put the new condenser in and tightened it down with the screwdriver, then did the same thing with the new points. "You don't tighten the points all the way down yet," he pointed out. "You have to adjust them first. How 'bout look through those feeler gauges and find me the sixteen one-thousandth."

Jack put the lug wrench back on the pulley nut. "We're gonna back off just a little bit here," he said, "to about 10 degrees before top dead center." He moved the white mark back to approximately the eleven o'clock position. I picked up the gauges, which looked kind of like a pocket knife with about a dozen little thin blades, and sorted through 'til I found one with .016 on it.

"Anyway," he continued with the story about Frankie, "he finally put a 'For Sale' sign on the car." I handed Jack the feeler gauge with the .016 blade extended. "Thanks," he said, "now look here."

I watched as he used the screwdriver to

make the points open and close slightly. Meanwhile, Jack slid the feeler blade between the ends of the points. "You should feel the blade *just* slide through," he said. "We call that gapping the points."

"Got it," I said.

"Then you tighten them down." And he did.

"So then you bought the car?" I asked.

"Well, actually, I felt kind of bad, so finally we told him what had been going on. But--well, you'd have to know Frankie, I guess--but he just couldn't admit anybody had pulled anything over on him. He said the car had other problems, anyway, and, by God, he was gonna sell it." Jack put the distributor cap back in place and snapped the clamps to hold it.

"So you bought it."

"I told him I'd buy it and keep it and sell it back to him if he changed his mind." Jack handed me the car keys. "Here," he said, "start it up and let's see if we need to adjust the timing."

"You want *me* to start it?" I was incredulous.

"Sure," he said, "just make sure it's in neutral. You know how, right?"

"I've started my dad's car," I said.

"No problem, then," Jack said.

I got in behind the steering wheel, sat

forward on the seat so that I could reach the pedals, and pulled back on the floor shifter until I felt it moving around freely in the neutral position. I put the key in the ignition. "Ready?" I called back to Jack.

"Fire 'er up," he called back. And I did.

"Give her a little gas," Jack said. I goosed the gas pedal a couple of times. "Okay--that's good," he said, "shut her down." And I turned it off. When I got out, Jack was gathering up his tools.

"That was pretty neat," I observed. "Is that it?" I handed him the keys.

Jack put the toolbox back in the trunk and closed the lid. "For now," he said.

"That didn't look too hard," I said.

"Some things you can fix," he said, "and some things, you can't." He came back and closed the engine cover. "I think I'm ready for a cold drink," Jack said. "Dr. Pepper or Cheerwine? You have any thoughts on that?"

"No, sir."

He pulled a rag from his back pocket and wiped his hands. "So if I were to say to you--'Slick, come on in and let me buy you a cold drink'--you wouldn't know which one you'd rather have?"

"Well," I said. "I'd probably go with the Cheerwine today."

"Any reason for that?" he asked.

"No sir," I replied. "That's just the first thought that came to my tastebuds."

"I see," he said. "Well, you've been a big help. Can I buy you a Cheerwine, then, as a token of my appreciation?"

"I didn't really do anything," I said. "You don't have to do that."

"Didn't say I had to," he picked up his clipboard from the roof of the car. "Just asked if I could. Or do you think your mom and dad might get mad?"

"No sir," I told him. "I don't reckon my momma and dad really care."

"Hmmm," he stuck the pencil from the clipboard into his shirt pocket, "maybe we ought to go inside and grab us a drink and just see if that helps anything at all." He headed inside. I followed. "Grab us a couple of Cheerwines out of the drink box," he said, as he went behind the counter and hung the clipboard on a nail in the wall beside the Hinckley Ford Company calendar.

I slid open the shiny top of the drink box and reached down inside, feeling for the coldest ones-- as if I could actually discern some deviation of a degree or two from one bottle to the next. Pulling out two cold ones, I hung them one after the other by their yellow metal bottle caps in the bucktoothed bottle opener on the front of the box, and chissssshthunk-chinked them open. I held mine under my nose and let the carbonation tickle my nose, as I crossed and set his on the counter.

"Here's to problems," Preacher Jack said, "may we have 'em a long, long time." And he raised his bottle in a kind of toast.

"Huh?" I said. "You *want* to have problems?"

"No, no, no," he said, "I don't *want* 'em. What I said was 'may we *have* 'em a long, long time.' See, as long as we're alive, we're gonna have problems--there's no getting around that--so...the longer we have problems, the longer we hang around this old green earth."

"You sure have some funny ways of puttin' things sometime," I said to him. "You know that?"

"I suppose I do," he said, and we both took a drink. "Problems at home?" he asked.

"How'd you know?" I asked.

"Just a wild guess," he said.

"Oh," I said, as if that was an actual explanation that I understood. "How can grown-ups know one day that they're supposed to be married, and then the next day know they're *not* supposed to be?"

He paused for a moment. I don't think that he was expecting quite that unwieldy a problem.

"Well...people change, Slick," he began.

"Doesn't mean it's anything you did or anything you can do anything about. And it surely doesn't mean they don't both still love you and want to look after you."

"How do I know that?" I asked. "I mean, if they knew last week that they loved each other and wanted to be married to each other, and this week they don't know that anymore, how do I know they won't change their minds about me next week?"

"Some things you just know, Slick."

"I ain't so sure about that," I said. "What if they forget they know that?"

"You don't have to remember what you *know*," he said.

"What's that mean?" I asked.

"You know how to walk, don't you?" he said.

"Yeah. I mean, yessir."

"You don't have to remember how every time, right?"

"Right."

"But can you tell me *how* you know how to do that?"

"I learned."

"Yeah, that's right, you did. You learned how to ride a bike, too, right?"

"Yessir."

"And that's even more complicated,

probably. So when I ask you--'Can you ride a bike?'--what do you say?"

"I say 'yessir, I can.'"

"But how do you *know*? I mean, what if you've forgotten how? It's not like we *are* riding bikes and I ask you. 'Cause if we're doing that, when I ask you if you can ride a bike, you just say, 'yeah--see?' 'Cause you see and you know. So you see, you can tell me that you knew how to ride a bicycle yesterday, and if we're riding now you can tell me you know how to ride one right this instant, but when it comes to tomorrow...how can you tell me that you'll still know how? ... You can't tell me how you know. You just know. Some things you just know."

I wondered if that's why Preacher Jack went into preaching--back when he did, I mean--because he had that way of explaining things so that you were left for a minute not knowing what to say because you were so busy thinking about what he'd just said. And so for about a minute I just sucked on the Cheerwine bottle, letting the vacuum pull my tongue inside. Then I pulled it out with a wet thunk.

"But how do you even know what you know when you listen to everything you thought you knew change in half an hour? Half an hour. One person says one thing, and then they both say a lot of things, and then one starts crying, and then the other starts crying, and then I start crying--and they're both so busy talking and crying that they both forgot I'm even there--right there in the next room--listening and crying--but then I'm so busy crying that I forget to listen and I must've missed something, and the next thing you know, my momma, she's gone. She's just gone. ... She didn't say goodbye. ... How does that happen? How do you even know what you know anymore after that?"

And then it was his turn to take a minute and just sip on his bottle. 'Course, he didn't suck all the air out of the minute like I did.

"If she doesn't come talk to you about it by this time tomorrow," he said, "your mom, I mean-- if she doesn't find a way to talk to you somehow about this...by this time tomorrow... I'll give you the store."

"Sir?" I said. "You'll do what?"

"Give you the store. What time is it?"

I looked up at the Dr. Pepper clock over the counter. All the numbers were bold black except for the 10, 2, and 4 that were yellow with bright red outlines.

"Nearly 8 o'clock," I said.

"The store, the gas station, the whole thing. I'll give you the whole thing if your mom doesn't talk to you about all this by 8 o'clock tomorrow night. ... I guess you better be thinking about what you're gonna do if you wind up with this place tomorrow."

"But what'll *you* do?" I asked. "I mean, if you don't have this place."

"Well," he said, "I guess that's what I better be thinking about. But, you know--it just seems to me...you gotta have faith in something, I think. ... Take that drink with you, Slick. You can bring the bottle back tomorrow if it's mine, or just keep it if it's yours."

I walked on home, nursing the Cheerwine and wondering what in the world I might do if I had my own store.

The next morning, when I woke up to the smell of my mother cooking breakfast, and I went in the kitchen, and she said we needed to talk, and we sat there and ate scrambled eggs and bacon and toast with grape jelly, and she told me what being separated was going to be like, I told her about what Preacher Jack had said. And that's when she cried.

"It's okay, Momma," I said, "I didn't want that ol' store, anyway." I put my arm around her and told her, "I'll take the bottle back after while." And I did.

# CHAPTER SIX

Preacher Jack ran his thumbnail along the perforated "Open Here" path of the box of coconut candy bars, lifted the flap, and folded it back to form a palm tree-festooned display at the top of the cellophaned pink and white and brown-striped planks of coconut candy.

I looked at the palm trees and asked, "How far's Florida from here?"

"Plannin' a vacation, Slick?" Jack replied.

"How far, do you reckon?" I repeated.

"You wouldn't want to drive there all in one day," he said. "I mean, if you could drive."

"Oh," I said and just left the empty O floating there in the air like a soap bubble for about the time it would've taken for it to settle to the floor and pop. Preacher Jack let it float on the silence, too. "I hear a guy can wander around in Florida and pick enough oranges and coconuts and grapefruits and other stuff right off trees, just right there along side the road--I mean, right there free for the takin'--to have plenty to eat even if he don't have a job or anything. And it's warm enough you don't even have to have a place to live, either."

"I never really thought of you as hobo material," Jack said, and rearranged the boxes of candy on the shelf.

I noticed he had slipped the Coconut Delights in between the Chock-O-Lots and Gobs-O-Nuts, and I realized that Preacher Jack had the candy arranged in alphabetical order. For just a second, I was tempted to see if other things were arranged alphabetically, too--the drinks in the cooler--did the Blenheim's Root Beer precede the Cheerwine, which came before the Coca-Cola, which gave way to Dr. Pepper, and right on down the line to YooHoo?--but I decided to save that for later.

"Do you think there still *are* hoboes," I asked.

"With a deal like you're talking about in Florida," Jack bobbed his head, "I don't see how there could *help* but be hoboes. Heck--I'm about half tempted myself."

"Oh," I said again.

I had a feeling that any hoboes who had actually given in to that temptation were not as personable as Preacher Jack, though. In fact, the hobo image in my head lived over in that area where the scary things resided--not right there on Monster Alley or Witches Way--but definitely somewhere in that neighborhood. I didn't relish the possibility of competing with them for my daily orange ration.

"You thinking about hitting the road?"

Preacher Jack asked.

"My mother says she wants me to come and live with her," I told him, "and my dad wants me to stay with him. They're gonna go to court and fight about it, I think."

"You think hitting the road's going to make them not fight or somehow change their minds about this whole separation thing, Slick?"

"I just thought I could go off on my own for a while maybe, and they'd see how dumb this whole thing is," I said.

"Well, yeah, you could do that, Slick," Preacher Jack said, "or there's another route you could take."

I told him I didn't supposed I had thought too hard about other routes. Except maybe one.

"What do you know about makin' deals with God?" I asked him. "I mean, do they teach you about that at preacher school?"

"I don't know that God's much of a deal-maker," he said. "but what kind of deal did you have in mind?"

"You think it'll jinx whatever chance I might have if I tell you about it?" I asked. "I mean, you not being a real preacher and all anymore."

"I think my not being a preacher anymore might actually work in your favor--if there was going to be any chance of a deal at all, I mean."

"Well," I began, "I did some stealing a while back. I never got caught or anything, and I wish I hadn't done it, but I did."

"Wishing you hadn't done it is a good sign, Slick,"

Preacher Jack rubbed his chin and sat down in one of the two unpainted, straight-back wooden chairs that sat near the drink box. He didn't tell me to sit down, too, or even nod at it with his head as an invitation to join him like he sometimes did, but even so, I walked over and sat down beside him. It just felt like the right thing to do.

Somebody had carved "FUCI" with the point of a knife, it looked like, in the plain wooden seat of the chair I sat in. It looked like whoever had done it had been interrupted before he could finish the "<" part of the K, and I had wondered a couple of times before who the knife-wielder might've been, and how he'd gotten as much of the carving done as he had, especially if it was done in the store there.

I decided it must've been done before Preacher Jack took over the store, and, whoever the carver was, he either hadn't had a chance to finish what he'd started since Jack took over, or he thought he'd probably better not take a chance on finishing such a dirty word now that the chair belonged to someone with Preacher Jack's connection with things holy--even if that connection seemed to be attenuated at the moment.

"This ain't tattlin' or anything," I added, "but you know my friend Gilbert, don't you?"

"Yeah," said Jack. "You stole something from Gilbert?"

"No sir," I continued, "I stole something *with* him."

"Uh huh," Jack nodded. "Co-conspirators."

"Does that make it worse?" I asked.

"I don't think so," he answered.

"My mother says we're a bad influence on each other, Gilbert and me. She says when we get together, we're just trouble lookin' for a place to happen."

That wasn't always the case, but the times it proved to be true produced the kinds of troubling incidents that stuck in people's memories. The previous summer, Gilbert and I both played on the same Little League team--the Myers Park Cardinals. It was Gilbert's last year of eligibility. A kid named Eddie Callahan played first base. Eddie chewed great wads of bubble gum and spit a lot, but everybody liked him. He bloused his uniform pants low--almost down to his ankles--and wore a St. Christopher's medal on a leather cord around his neck for good luck.

In what had to be one of the freakiest

accidents of all time, Eddie accidentally hanged himself. The story was that the family dog was in the basement and started barking, and Eddie's mother told him to go check on the dog. Apparently, as he started down the stairs--wooden, poorly lighted, and with no handrail--Eddie must've fallen. The leather cord around his neck caught on a slightly raised nail head on one of the steps, and that was it. When the dog continued to bark--even more urgently now--Eddie's mother went to check and found him. But it was too late.

It was an awful, tragic, heart-breaking story among the parents, and we kids were upset, as well, but we didn't have enough experience with death yet--its permanence, its impact on the survivors--to know really how to deal with it. So, by and large, we didn't deal with it. We were appropriately sad, but that was about all.

My mother offered to take us to the funeral-- the entire team was going, but not *as* a team--our parents were bringing us individually, or in twos and threes. The parents were going anyway for Eddie's parents' sake. When we got to the church, everybody was filing past the open casket down front, then going to their seats in the pews to await the beginning of the service.

As we stood in line--Gilbert, me, and my mom--and the line moved slowly closer to the casket, I began to feel an uneasiness I had never felt before. I wasn't sure what it was or why I was feeling it. Finally, we got to the front and paused before the open casket. It was my first encounter with a dead body. Gilbert and I both stood and looked at the strangely Eddie-like body lying there for a few seconds. We turned and looked at each other and--inexplicably--burst into laughter. I can't imagine why. It was just awful. It was like somehow the emotions got all mixed up in our minds, and when it all bubbled over, it came out as laughter.

My mother, of course, was mortified. And furious. She grabbed each of us by the backs of our shirts and whisked us out of the church. I don't remember what she said. It didn't matter. We had no defense. We had no explanation. We had nothing except the most damning proof yet that she was right--that we were just trouble lookin' for a place to happen.

"Well, a while back," I continued to Jack, "me and Gilbert were in the Western Auto, and we were lookin' at the stuff in the fishing tackle area. They've got an awful lot of neat stuff there, ya know."

"I'm not sure who thinks it's neater," Jack offered, "the fish or the fishermen."

"I don't know, either," I said, "but I was

looking at this rod and reel, and Gilbert came over to me and said, 'Psst. Look what I got,' and motioned with his head for me to look at his right jacket pocket. He had his hand in his pocket, and when I looked down, he pulled his hand part way out of his pocket, and he had a big 'ol yellow and red lure still in the plastic case. He shoved his hand, along with the lure, back into his pocket, and bumped me with his elbow, and said, 'Now you get one.' I said, 'No!'--'course I said it real low 'cause I just knew we were gonna get caught and both end up in reform school, and I looked around to see if anybody else had seen, but nobody was even paying any attention to us. So I said real low again, 'Put it back, Gilbert. And let's get outa here.' 'Come over here with me,' he said, 'stand in the way so they don't see me put it back.' So I followed him over to where the lures were. There musta been a thousand different ones--purple and gold ones, blue and silver ones, some green ones with scales painted on 'em, plastic worms, bucktails, flies, spinners, spoons, and some yellow and red ones, of course, like the one Gilbert had in his pocket. 'Turn around and watch out for me,' he said, and so I turned around and was trying to act like I wasn't doing anything--which is really hard to do when you really are doing something, especially something you're not supposed to be doing--and the next thing I knew, I felt Gilbert stick something in my pocket. I tried not to look, but I knew what it was, and just as I was starting to say something and take it out of my pocket, one of the salesmen came around the end of the aisle and said, 'Findin' everything you need, boys?' I...I couldn't say anything, but Gilbert said, 'Y'all got BBs?' and the man said they did but they kept 'em behind the counter. Gilbert put his hand in his pocket and pulled out some change and looked at it and said, 'I guess we'll have to come back later, anyway' and kinda bumped me and said, 'Come on, let's go.' And we just walked right out without payin' or nothin'."

"Sounds to me like you weren't so much a thief as an unwitting accomplice," said Jack. I guess he could tell by the way I looked at him that I didn't know what that was, so he added, "Sounds like you didn't really mean to steal anything."

"But I did, didn't I?"

"Well, yeah--technically, I guess you did."

"That's what I thought. At least that's what it felt like. But it gets worse," I went on. "After we got out of the store and down the road a little ways, I told Gilbert, 'What the h-- ... What're you *doin'*?!' And he just laughed. He thought it was a hoot! I took the lure out of my pocket and threw it at him and told him to keep it--that I didn't want it, and to *never* do that again. He just kept on laughin' and callin' me a wuss and chicken and stuff like that. He kept it up all afternoon 'til I went home."

"You went back, didn't you?" Preacher Jack asked.

"How'd you know?" I asked him.

"I could see it coming. Besides," he said, "you said it got worse."

"He just kept bringin' it up for the next several days, and callin' me a chicken and wussy-boy and stuff. Finally, just to shut him up I told him I'd do it. It was maybe a week later. We went in, and I just went straight to the fishin' stuff and looked around to see that nobody was lookin' and grabbed a little box of split-shot weights and stuck 'em in my pocket and walked out. After I got outside, I started runnin'. Gilbert was still in the store, but I just left him and ran. Down the road, I stopped and waited on him. When he finally came walking up, I pulled out the split-shots and said, 'There! I got 'em. See! Ya happy now?' And he just laughed and reached in his pocket and pulled out a fish scaler and a pack of flashlight batteries and said, 'I got the batteries while the guy was gettin' BBs from behind the counter.' Then he showed me the tube of BBs that he actually bought. I think he's probably still doin' it--stealing stuff from the Western Auto. He stole a pack of cigarettes one time from the grocery store, too."

"And how about you?" Preacher Jack got up from his chair and went and straightened some boxes of saltine crackers on one of the shelves, like they had gotten out of line to listen to us while we were talking.

"I never did it again," I said. "But still once you've stole stuff, you don't know if you might do it again or not."

Preacher Jack looked at me a few seconds, like he could tell maybe from the way I was sitting or something, and said, "I don't expect you will."

"Well," I said, "what I told God in my deal-- I mean I was prayin' and all when I made the deal-- was that if He'd fix it so my momma would come back home, I'd never steal anything again."

"I see," Jack nodded. "What'd you do with the split-shots?"

"I threw 'em in the creek," I said.

"Well," he said, "I don't pretend to speak for God or anything, but I suspect He already knows you won't do it again."

"Does that mean we don't have a deal?" I asked.

"That's the thing," Jack smiled, "you just never know whether you've got a deal or not."

He walked to the door and looked out, and neither one of us said anything for a minute. "I had a friend," he said, "back when I was a young man.

His name was Vick. In those days we were both pretty much what folks around here would call heathens. Far as we were concerned, Friday and Saturday nights were only made for two things. One of 'em was drinking beer, and...you're still not quite old enough for me feel comfortable talking to you about what the other was."

"Was it floozies?" I asked, straight-faced and serious as a ministerial counselor.

Preacher Jack smiled. "Well, they weren't any floozier than we were, I don't suppose, but-- yes--that's probably about the way a lot of people looked at it at the time. Anyway, you got the right idea."

"You tellin' me you once drank beer and ran around with floozies, Preacher Jack?"

I was having trouble picturing him in that role at all. I had seen the people who hung out down at the Red Bird Cafe. The Red Bird, as they called it, was a honky-tonk, and though I'd never been inside, of course, something inside me, I felt, buzzed at the same frequency as the neon lights that lighted the front of the joint at night. And when we passed and it was alive with bent bright neon and the crowd-noise-filtered sound of jukebox music, I watched it and its population of drunks and floozies--as my mother referred to them--with a sense of forbidden excitement that I knew I wasn't supposed to be feeling. It made me think of a passage in *Treasure Island* when Jim first sees the pirates and he knows what he's seeing is dangerous and wicked and he shouldn't even look, much less want to venture closer, but he can't help himself, and I wanted to stowaway inside The Red Bird and see it all and hear it all and feel it all close up for just one night.

The closest I'd ever gotten, though, was a hot, rainy July night when we got caught in traffic stopped on the road that ran past The Red Bird. We stopped almost right in front, and my dad said there must've been a bad accident, and my mom said she hoped nobody got hurt, and I sat in the back seat and looked through the rain-streaked glass at The Red Bird, looking like it was melting in the rain. There were men and women--drunks and floozies, I supposed--lined up just under the eves along the front of the building, standing beneath a cloud of cigarette smoke of their own making, each with a bottle or a can in his or her hand, and almost all of them staring off at whatever was going on at the front of the line of idling cars. We had the windows about halfway down as we sat there, trying to find that balance between letting a breeze in and keeping the rain out.

Suddenly, a man appeared at my dad's open window. His hair was plastered down and his face wet with rain, his eyes squinted--as much to keep out the smoke of the damp cigarette he clenched between his teeth as to keep out the rain. He hadn't shaved in a couple of days, and there was a smell about him that I instinctually knew was what a weekend steeped in beer must smell like. My God, it was a Red Bird drunk standing right there by our car!

He said, "Motorcycle wreck," at the same time my mother said to my father, "Roll up the window," and my dad said, "What?" as much to one as to the other, I guess, and they both said their lines simultaneously again, only this time the Red Bird drunk added, "It's a bad 'un," and that was enough to override my mother's admonition.

While she was busy rolling up the rest of the windows and making sure the doors were all locked, my dad asked, "Anybody hurt?"

"Junior Crowder," the drunk said--"You know him?"

"I know *of* him," my dad replied.

"It's nasty," the Red Bird drunk went on. "Got pinned under his motorcycle and the rear wheel was still spinning and it just ate his guts right out. 'S nasty."

"Roll up the window!" my mother said again, and this time my father knew she meant it.

"Thanks," my dad said to the man as he

rolled the window up.

For a moment the Red Bird drunk just stood there in the rain like he didn't understand why he hadn't been invited in to discuss the accident in detail, then he turned and walked back toward the car that was stopped behind us. I watched him stop in front of the driver's window, then my mother told me to turn around and keep my eyes straight ahead. And there we sat in the quiet sweltering night and listened to the rhythmic slap and bump of the windshield wipers 'til the line of cars started to move forward.

Up ahead, when we passed the flashing red lights and the knot of people standing in the rain by the side of the road, I knew my dad wanted to look as much as I did, but we didn't slow down. We just drove on by. But I took with me the picture in my head of the motorcycle eating Junior Crowder's guts out, and I took with me the picture of the only Red Bird drunk I'd ever seen close up. Preacher Jack didn't look anything like him.

"Vick was a better sort than people gave him credit for being," said Preacher Jack. "'Course he's not the first one that's happened to. He started seeing this young lady pretty serious--they were talking about getting married and all. Some things happened--I'm not going to try to explain them all to you at this point--but he took her to see this doctor."

"She was sick?" I asked.

"She had a condition," Preacher Jack said. "A condition she couldn't go to one of the doctors around where we lived for."

"Was he a specialist?" I said.

"Well...he was a doctor who took care of special problems, let's say. Turned out he wasn't a very good doctor, either. And the procedure he performed..."

"Procedure?" I interrupted.

"Operation," Jack continued, "...the operation he performed caused her to get worse, and she died. Vick, he just went all to pieces. Never was the same. A lot of people blamed him, and even worse, he blamed himself. He started drinking way, way too much, and after a while, he had what folks call a nervous breakdown."

"You mean he went crazy?"

"Sort of," Preacher Jack said, though it didn't look like he was very comfortable with the term. "And one night, he got real drunk, it seems, and went out to this place outside of town--a railroad crossing that was far enough out that the train had picked its speed back up after coming through town--and he parked his truck and got out and walked a good ways down the railroad track and sat and drank some more. The train engineer said he was crawling down the middle of the track on his hands and knees when he saw him, and, there was no time to even slow down, much less stop."

I felt my eyes get big. "He got run over by the train?"

"He did, Slick. He got as run over by a train as you can get," said Jack. "And it was his funeral, I guess, that made me start thinking about different routes."

I shifted around to get comfortable. "What happened?"

"You ever heard anything about what happens to people who kill themselves? I mean, what happens to their souls?" asked Jack.

I thought a few seconds and reckoned I hadn't heard anything. Or if I had, I didn't remember.

"There are folks--church folks--preachers and such--who'll tell you that if someone kills himself, his soul goes to hell."

"Why?" I asked.

"'Cause killing yourself's just that bad a sin, as far as those folks are concerned."

"Is that what the Bible says?" I asked.

Preacher Jack stopped and looked like he was about to start off down a whole 'nother story path, but then changed his mind. "You know the commandment that says 'Thou shalt not kill,' don't

75

you?"

I said that I did, and immediately heard shouts in my head and felt just inside my shoulder blades the icy tingle that some remembering brings. It had been two years ago--back when Gilbert was still a kid and didn't mind acting like one.

It was every bit as hot as I imagined Florida got, and we had stripped down to our underpants and fashioned loincloths from a couple of old towels. We had decided that if you mixed finger-paints with spit what you got was much closer to actual war paint than what you got if you mixed it with plain water out of the faucet.

I had two horizontal lines on my forehead--one red, one blue--a diagonal stripe on each cheek--red on the left cheek, blue on the right--and two short vertical stripes on my chin--this time blue on the left and red on the right. A long blue diagonal line and a long red diagonal line formed an X on my hairless chest. And I was called True Arrow.

Gilbert had a wavy blue line across his forehead, and red spots on his nose, his chin, and on each cheek. Blue wavy vertical lines down his chest alternated with rows of red dots. And he was called Spotted Snake. I started to say something to him about there not being any actual snakes with spots that I ever heard of, but realizing that under that war paint still beat the heart of Gilbert, I decided to let it go.

As small as our scouting party was--for that is what we decided we were--Spotted Snake decided that we still needed structure--a chain of command--and he dubbed himself head scout. Now that we were organized, we slipped, in true scout fashion, out of the yard and into the woods.

Spotted Snake forded the creek and signaled me to follow. In careful heel-toe stealth step, we moved from tree to tree to rock to bush until we approached Flint Cave. Flint Cave was not a cave at all. It was a slightly concave sheer rock cliff. Boulders on either side of the cliff funneled approachers to the craggy dead end. We decided that we would sort through the flint rocks that covered the ground at the foot of the cliff for suitable arrowheads and spear points, and as we brushed through the bushes at the edge of the clearing, we flushed a rabbit.

The startled animal and the startled scouting party had exactly opposite reactions initially-- Spotted Snake and I jumped, then froze; the rabbit jumped and ran...directly into the rocky cul-de-sac. Once we realized that what had leapt out was only a rabbit, we took off after it.

Spotted Snake dashed ahead, and the frightened creature raced straight to the base of the cliff, then scrambled to the left, looking for an escape route. Spotted Snake grabbed a handful of rocks and began throwing them in front of the rabbit's path.

"Cut 'im off! Get some rocks!" the head scout shrieked.

As the rocks smacked the wall in front of it, the terrified animal reversed itself and scampered back along the wall in the other direction. Caught up in the thrill of the hunt, I picked up several rocks and began to fling them at the scurrying furball.

"Box 'im in! Get 'im!" Spotted Snake howled.

And then we both were snatching up rocks and slinging them, whooping and laughing, caught up in the frenzy of our own cruel, yet naive savagery until I side-armed an Easter egg-sized rock that ricocheted once and caught the panicked creature in the side. The rabbit jerked into the air and came down on its side; its body and legs spasmed. I froze.

"You got 'im! You got 'im!" my fellow savage shouted. "Come on!" he moved in for the kill. He hurled an especially big stone at the twitching creature, and it landed with a terrible thud.

The rabbit lay still. Spotted Snake stood right over it and pelted it with another and another and another rock. The clearing was quiet now except for the sound of Gilbert's ruthless rocks.

I stood there in the heat and the overkill, my war paint streaked, running, and realized I was crying. When Gilbert stopped, he looked at me, and for several long moments neither of us knew what to say. Finally, Gilbert straightened up, and threw down the couple of rocks he still held in his hand; he made a noise that was two parts sneer and one part laugh, and started walking back into the woods, back towards my house, back towards civilization. I wiped my face with my sweaty forearm and sniffed hard and followed him.

"It doesn't just mean don't kill somebody else," Preacher Jack said. "It means don't kill yourself either. Some people believe that breaking commandments--especially without ever repenting, without asking forgiveness and all--gets you sent to Hell. And if you kill yourself, well, you certainly don't have the chance to do any repenting."

"Couldn't you do your repenting in advance?" I asked.

"You ask a lot of preachers that, Slick, and you got yourself a whole 'nother sermon," he replied. "Anyway...at the funeral, there were two preachers that showed up. The first one seemed convinced that Vick was burning in eternal Hell already, and that the only good to come out of Vick's life at all was that he could serve as a bad

79

example to the rest of us--somebody to point at and say, 'You wanna end up in Hell like *him*?' 'Course even the family members who'd said for years that Vick was going to Hell in a handbag if he didn't change his ways weren't really ready, I don't think, to hear a preacher, a man of God, pronouncing that Vick was sure-enough *there*."

"Why do you suppose there's such a place as...down there?" I asked. I wasn't allowed to say Hell yet. At least not around grown-ups. Even if they'd been saying it themselves.

"It seems to me, Slick, that there are some folks who feel a need to pass judgment on other people and other people's lives--who want to punish other people for the way they live their lives. And if those other people are bad enough, in the minds of those folks who are doing the judging, they'd like to think there's some way to punish them beyond what's possible in this world. So they had to have some place of eternal punishment to accommodate the farthest reaches of their punishment imaginings."

"And those preachers at your friend Vick's funeral hated him that much?" I said, because even though I didn't fully understand everything Preacher Jack had just said, what I did catch sounded an awful lot like hate to me.

"I don't think it's that they hated him so

much as it was that they loved the idea of a place as bad as Hell. People-judging is a curious activity. The other preacher I told you was there?--he was what I've come to think of as the loophole guy."

I allowed that I didn't have a clue what a loophole was, much less a loophole guy.

"The loophole guy--Preacher Number Two-- he had a theory. He had come up with a scenario of the way the whole thing *might've* happened and in *his* version of what might've happened, Vick *might* not have actually killed himself--in fact, it might've been an accident."

"A real accident, or accidentally-on-purpose?" I asked.

"Hmmph--I think you're starting to get the idea of what a loophole is all about," said Jack. "Preacher Number Two said that he'd heard from somebody that the engineer on the train had said that when he saw Vick on the tracks, Vick was up on his hands and knees, like he was crawling, or trying to crawl, at least. Then Preacher Number Two went on to say that that sounded to him like a man who'd changed his mind about being out there on them tracks--like a man who was trying to crawl off them tracks, out of the way of that train. And, if that was the case, Vick had had time, just as that train was bearing down on him, to ask God to forgive him--to admit he'd made a mistake and to realize the error of his ways and to ask for forgiveness. Preacher Number Two said it only took an instant to be forgiven--that it could happen in a flash--and that's what he thought might've happened, and that's what he thought the family ought to think happened. That Vick was saved from Hell at the last second."

"And that's the loophole?" I asked.

"That's the loophole," Preacher Jack nodded.

"You reckon that's true?" I said. "You reckon that's what happened?"

"I suspect that what Preacher Number Two thought he was doing was that he was somehow comforting the family. That he was sort of striking some kind of deal for Vick. But, no," said Preacher Jack, "no, I don't think Vick was trying to get away or that he was doing any last second repenting."

"Does that mean you think your friend really did go to...down there?"

"No, Slick," Preacher Jack said, "I don't think he went to Hell at all."

"Why not?" I asked.

"'Cause I'm not so sure there really is an eternal Hell," Preacher Jack said. "As far as Vick was concerned, I suspect he thought he was *leaving* Hell on that train."

I told Preacher Jack that I thought that was a

mighty strange thing for a preacher to believe, much less say out loud. He asked me back if it was any less strange coming from a guy who ran a gas station. I told him I guessed that, even though he was running a gas station, I still thought of him as a preacher... kind of.

"And even though my friend Vick sat down on a railroad track and got run over by a train, I guess I still think of him as a pretty good guy, kind of. And I'd like to think that, if there is a place like Hell, you've gotta be a whole lot worse than a pretty good guy to get sent there," said Jack. "And when it comes to making deals," he added, "you don't do what's right because of what God might do for you, or do *to* you. You do what's right because it just doesn't make sense in this world to do any other way."

I thought about it a minute and said I reckoned that what he thought made a lot more sense than what a lot of other people thought.

"That 'thou shall not kill' thing--" I added, "--that's talking about people, isn't it? I mean, it don't mean animals, does it?"

"It means people, I think, mostly," Jack said, "but maybe not entirely. Depends. Why?"

"No reason," I told him. "I was just wondering, was all."

# CHAPTER SEVEN

"They each got another one yesterday," I said.

"Yeah--I listened to the game on the radio," Jack said, but he didn't look up from the ledger book he was writing in.

"That was number 350 career home run for Mantle," I said.

"That's what they say," Jack flipped back a few pages in the book and studied something on the page.

"He hit if off Early Wynn." I stood there and waited for Jack to respond, but he just kept reading. "My dad played baseball with Early Wynn in high school," I added, sure that would get his attention.

Jack opened a cigar box and took out a couple of invoices. I couldn't believe he didn't recognize the impressiveness of the connection. I was the son of the man who played high school baseball with the guy who threw the pitch that Mickey Mantle hit for his 350th home run. Wow. Jack kept looking back and forth between the invoices and the ledger book. I couldn't believe it. I turned to leave, and Jack looked up.

"Did you need something, Slick?" he asked, just like he hadn't heard anything I'd told him.

"My dad played baseball with Early Wynn,"

I said, leaving him to fill in the blanks, and it would serve him right if he couldn't.

"Oh," he said, "I didn't know that."

"I know," I said. "You workin' on something there?" I nodded at the ledger book.

I had a notebook that looked just like it. I used it for my drawings, most of which turned into variations on the same theme--a battle in which Confederate soldiers, inexplicably armed with modern weaponry, defended the world against alien invaders complete with flying saucers. Unfortunately, I was long on imagination and short on both talent and technique. I really wanted to be able to draw. I wanted to be able to look at something and pick up a pencil or a paintbrush and re-create that vision on paper. Maybe it was the influence of a short lifetime of *Saturday Evening Post* covers, I don't know, but as far as I was concerned, Norman Rockwell was the god of drawing. I could feel myself almost stepping into some of his pictures. I came to know some of the faces he drew almost as well as I knew the faces of some people in town. They were absolutely real.

One of the guys in my class at school last year could draw. I mean, he could *really* draw. Andy could draw a picture of one of the girls in class, and it would look just like her. He could draw a picture of a car that looked like it came right off the front of one of those model car boxes. And he didn't even look like he was trying. He just...did it.

It was while I was watching Andy effortlessly whip out one of those picture-perfect drawings that it occurred to me that, if you really, really wanted to do something--I mean, if you really thought about it hard enough--concentrated--you ought to be able to just...do it. Whatever it was. Draw a picture. Play the piano. Smack homeruns. Fly! I mean, actually flap your arms and fly!

It just seemed to me that if you wanted to do whatever it was strongly enough, you ought to be able to do it. Suddenly. Magically. It was, I thought, a sound theory and well within the realm of possibility.

Based purely on that theory, I crept up on several unsuspecting pianos and forced them to produce terrible, discordant noises. I ran, flapping, across my back yard and later thought how fortunate it was for me that I didn't live near the Grand Canyon. I rationalized after each failure of the theory to prove itself in whatever effort I had most recently undertaken that I simply had not concentrated hard enough--that the theory was still fundamentally valid--in theory--that the flaw was merely in my application of the theory.

I decided that Mantle and Maris had somehow tapped into the theory--that they, too, had figured out that if they concentrated--if they really, really wanted the ball to meet the fat part of the bat--to thwack exactly into the sweet spot--and to go rocketing off into the upper deck of right field--that...it would! At some level, I decided, Mickey and Roger and I *knew*. We shared the secret of the theory. But I wasn't going to try to explain it all to Jack right then--with his books and bills and papers spread out everywhere.

"I just can't decide," Jack said, "which I'm worse at--preaching or storekeeping."

I didn't have an answer for him right then. "They're playin' the White Sox again today," I said.

"Yeah," he nodded, "you going to listen to it?"

"Probably," I answered.

"You sure you don't need anything?" Jack asked, but he still had the book open and the invoices spread out on the counter.

"Nah," I said, "I just thought I'd stop by."

I pushed open the screen door and let it slap shut behind me as I left. I decided I might go by Gilbert's house, then I stopped, extended my arms, cupped my hands, and moved my arms up and down a couple of times. The Wright Brothers had used a hill--Kill Devil Hills to help launch their flying machine. I thought of a hill in a field at the edge of the woods, changed my mind about

Gilbert's house, and headed towards the woods.

# CHAPTER EIGHT

Gilbert eyed my Dr. Pepper. "You get that at Preacher Jack's store?"

"Yeah. You want to go get one?" I asked.

"Ol' Lady Enslow at church told my momma that Preacher Jack ain't nothin' but a heathen, an' he's goin' to hell in a hand basket," said Gilbert. "I'd be careful 'f I was you about hangin' around too much with somebody who's goin' to hell in a hand basket."

"Miss Enslow thinks everybody's going to hell who doesn't jump when she says jump."

"Yeah, but he's a heathen sure enough. Everybody says so," Gilbert added.

I took a drink of Dr. Pepper and watched Gilbert out of the corner of my eye. I lowered the bottle and a small burp burned my nose.

"Preacher Jack's not any heathen. He was a preacher, for Pete's sake. You can't be both."

"Maybe he *turned* heathen," Gilbert curled his lip when he said it.

"He hadn't turned into nothing'," I said.

"Yeah? Then why'd he say what he said about us bein' God and God bein' us--like God wasn't even in heaven where He's always been, like God wasn't no better than us, huh?"

"He didn't say that."

"Yeah, he did, practically just like that. Even my mom said it was blast-a-mus."

The hand fans from Frost's Funeral Home stopped that last  morning that Preacher Jack had preached--like they had all been running on the same circuit and somebody had pulled the plug.

"Though I have made my own genuine peace with the Christian belief system," Preacher Jack began, "I have become increasingly *un*peaceful with the way it is being preached and perpetuated by just about everybody, including myself."

A few of the fans picked back up, but at about twice the speed as before. Frost's Funeral Home provided the fans free to the church, though I'm sure whatever investment went into those cardboard rectangles with the rounded corners and the wooden stick handles had been more than recovered by those among the congregation who in their sudden and separate griefs had remembered those cardboard scenes depicting lambs and lions lying down together in plush green pastures with Jesus standing beside them with His hand outstretched as if gesturing to the somber lettering that spelled out "Frost's Funeral Home--Here When You Need Us Most."

I always wanted to call Frost's and say, "Can y'all come over right away? I've got lambs and lions all over my front yard!" But somehow it seemed bad luck to make a prank phone call to a funeral home.

"Now I'm not even going to get started," Preacher Jack continued, "trying to deal with the whole mess of how this has all led to such an artificial pecking order of who's better than who, based on who has what or who has what color skin or who has the most money in the bank or who has suffered the most for the longest time, because I just can't sort it out any more. But let me just give you my take on the whole thing in a nutshell: God is in every one of us and every one of us is part of God. We are the sensory receptors of God. We are the nerve endings of God. We are the brain cells of God. I don't know about you, but I can't sort my nerves and brain cells that finely--to be able to rank them in some order of least to best. For those of you who think you can, though...just go ahead and rank me among the least."

The Popowski family had moved to town for no good reason that anybody could figure. They didn't have any relatives around here. They didn't have any friends that lived here and invited them to move down. Mr. Popowski wasn't transferred down here because of his job. In fact, when they first got here, neither Mr. nor Mrs. Popowski even *had* a job. They told somebody that they just got tired of the winters up north and so they moved south. It wasn't a good enough explanation for a lot of folks.

They had a son named Geoff. We asked him if he didn't think it was easier to just spell it the way it sounded, the way everybody else spelled it--Jeff-- but he said his folks had named him after somebody and the somebody they'd named him after had that funny spelling so there was nothing he could really do about it. We told him he'd better get used to having people spell his name wrong a lot, and he said he'd already gotten used to it before they even moved here. Other than that funny-spelled name, he was an all right kid. Giving their kid a funny-spelled name, though, wasn't the only odd way of thinking the Popowskis had.

They bought Clarence Brown's old service station just outside of town. Yep--the same place that went on to become the Pump-n-Preach. The place had just sat there since ol' Mr. Clarence Brown died. Mr. Brown had been a widower for more than ten years before he died. His daughter, Lana Gayle, had married an insurance salesman who had gotten transferred to somewhere in Mississippi, and his son, Ira Lee, had become a successful chiropractor in Charlotte, so neither of them was interested in running a gas station after their father died. And so the place just sat there for a long time.

The weeds and the rust probably thought

they'd won and that the place was theirs when the Popowskis came along. It was in the final stages of the fixing up that the odd way of thinking had revealed itself. The Popowskis had sunk just about every dime they had into fixing up the old place and getting it ready to open. They'd stocked some grocery items and cold drinks in, and the gas tanks were filled up, and Mr. Popowski had gone into town to Dickerson's Hardware Store to get a few items to make a "Grand Opening" sign. As he was checking out, Mr. Popowski snapped his fingers in that way people do when they remember something they'd forgotten, and he asked Mr. Dickerson if he had any restroom signs. Mr. Dickerson left Mr. Popowski standing there at the register and walked about halfway down the first aisle to where the signs were, and when he came back he set four small metal signs down on the counter.

They looked like license plates only smaller, and instead of letters and numbers that didn't really spell anything, there were two--raised black letters against white backgrounds--one of which read "Men" and another which read "Ladies." The third sign was also black letters on a white background, and it said "Restrooms In Rear." The fourth sign, though, had white letters on a black background. It read simply, "White Only."

Later on, some folks said that if Mr.

Popowski had just kept his mouth shut, had just taken all four of the signs and nailed up the three he wanted and just thrown the other one away, nobody'd probably have been any the wiser--not for a while, at least.

But Mr. Popowski didn't keep his mouth shut. He opened it right up and said, "I don't need that one," and pointed right at the "White Only" sign. Mr. Dickerson said later that he was just trying to be helpful, just trying to educate Mr. Popowski to the way things were.

Mr. Dickerson said, "If you don't put the sign up, they'll pester you to death asking if they can use your facility, and you'll have to tell every one of 'em 'no' individually."

"Who?" Mr. Popowski asked.

"Well, the coloreds, of course," Mr. Dickerson answered. It was Mr. Popowski's "Why would I tell them 'no'?" that did it, though. It was somewhere around the tenth telling of the story that Mr. Dickerson added the part about the cash register coming up eight dollars short, too--but by then that was just overkill. The Popowskis' investment--the place into which they'd sunk their every dime--was dead in the water. Even before somebody painted "Nigger Lover" across the front of the store.

Nobody ever said who did the actual painting, but Preacher Jack had walked up on several of the men at church talking about it. They were laughing, and one of the men said something about "the stupid Po-lock" only getting what he had coming to him.

"And that, friends, is all the sermonizing you will ever have to put up with from me. I seem to be fresh out of sermons." There was absolute silence as Preacher Jack walked up the aisle and out the double doors in back, and there was absolute silence for about ten seconds after the door closed. And then it got real noisy in there.

Preacher Jack picked up the place, basically, for the price of the gasoline in the storage tanks. Nobody was real sure where the Popowskis moved; they didn't seem to have much reason to leave a forwarding address.

## CHAPTER NINE

Since I was out of school for the summer and home all day, my dad hired a woman--in the vernacular of the day, a colored lady--to watch me. Or to be at the house, at least, so I wouldn't be left alone while he was at work. She wasn't a mammy or a maid--though she did clean up a little and wash and iron clothes. She was Miss Sarah. She was plump and, I'm guessing, middle-aged, and she smelled of spray starch and vanilla extract. And I was to mind her. That much was clear. Mostly I did.

The biggest exception was her constant admonishment that I was not to go to the woods. I was never sure exactly where that caution came from. I had gone to play in the woods and around the creek all my life. I couldn't imagine that my father had told her that I was not to go. Momma wasn't a big fan of me going to the woods--again, I'm not sure why--perhaps some kind of recessive fairy tale lessons of bad things lurking there--and occasionally when I would leave to go out to play and she would ask where I was going, and I would answer, "the woods," she would tell me no. But that was usually by way of some sort of punishment for something I'd done, some misbehavior for which I should be denied something I wanted to do--not really a labeling of the woods itself as "off limits." I suspected that my mother may have offered the kibosh on the woods up to Miss Sarah at some point as an appropriate penalty if I should misbehave myself--something to be withheld to keep me in line--and somehow it got twisted around in the communication process. However it happened, it was a daily admonition, and almost daily, I ignored it. Otherwise, what Miss Sarah said...went.

This was my fifth and final summer of having to deal with "the reading list," too.

Beginning the summer following first grade, and each summer until the sixth grade, we got a card on which we were to list the books we read over the summer vacation. The card had twelve lines. Twelve books. One per week. Years later, I would try to remember the reward for having filled up the card--the incentive--and finally it hit me. There was none. No reward. It was simply what was expected. It was what one did.

There may have been some vague, implied threat of being "set back" a grade if you failed to do the summer reading, but though we all knew a kid or two who had not been promoted to the next grade, none of us knew of anyone who was actually set back a grade specifically for not filling up his summer reading card.

At the beginning of the new school year, the new teacher would ask us to bring in our cards, and we would, and she would take them up. There was always some kid who would repeatedly "forget" to bring his card in until the teacher just stopped asking, but nothing disastrous ever befell him directly for the shortcoming--none that we ever saw, anyway.

But, we suspected it somehow was reflected on your Permanent Record--that deadly serious, obscure dossier that existed somewhere in the musty, dusty catacombs of public education. Heaven help the kid who had some black mark etched upon his Permanent Record. One could only speculate what sort of life one could expect to live after such a blemish was officially recorded for posterity.

Along with the warnings about playing in the woods, Miss Sarah reminded me a couple of times a week about my summer reading list. I had a few titles written on the card, but I was clearly behind the one-book-a-week schedule. The bookmobile from the public library came around twice a week during the summer. After the first couple of weeks, Miss Sarah began to talk about the embarrassing prospect of taking me by the hand and picking out a book for me.

My bent that summer was toward biographies, though I slipped in a Hardy Boys mystery and a book about snakes that was mostly pictures. One day at lunch, while I was eating the egg salad sandwich that Miss Sarah had prepared, she said, "Did you read your book for this week?"

"No, ma'am," I answered, "not yet."

She got up and went and got my most recent, and as yet untouched selection, *Young George Washington: Boy Hero*. "Why don't you read me a little bit," she said.

"Out loud?" I asked.

"Yes," she said, "You read me a little bit out of your book, and I'll see if I can find some banana puddin' for desert."

Banana pudding was a mighty fine inducement. I picked up the book. "Don't you know how to read for yourself?" I asked, and then immediately regretted asking when I saw the look on her face.

"Well, 'course I know how to read, honey"-- she called me honey a lot--"I know how to read just fine. But it's always nice to have somebody read you a story."

I opened the book and began to read aloud. Over the next several weeks, we also read about Squanto, and Davy Crockett, and Knute Rockne, and Lou Gehrig, and a fictional kid called *Shorty Gilstrap: Sparkplug of the Red Birds* about a boy who played shortstop for a Little League team.

A couple of times I'd get hung up on a

word, and I'd point to it and ask Miss Sarah, "What word is that?"

"Well," she'd say, "what does it *sound* like?" and I'd sound it out, and she'd tell me what it meant. I suppose what she told me was correct. It always seemed to make sense.

One week, I picked out a book about George Washington Carver. I suppose I thought I was picking it out for her. It's funny how some of the most instructive things in life can also be the most subtle.

Sometimes Miss Sarah would interrupt me to ask, "Why do you suppose he did that?"--usually after somebody in the story would do something— something odd, like George Washington chopping down a cherry tree, maybe--something like that-- never questioning whether it actually *happened* or not, just *why* the character did what he did--and we'd talk about it. I asked her about it one time--if she believed something in one of the stories had really happened--and she told me, "Truth is a powerful spice, honey. You only have to add a pinch of it to a story to make the made-up part taste just as real as the rest."

I recall learning *how* to read before I ever started first grade, but that summer, sitting at the kitchen table reading aloud to Miss Sarah, I learned what it meant really *to read*. I don't guess I ever told her that. But I'd like to think she knew.

# Chapter Ten

One Saturday afternoon after I had finished cutting the grass, I was streaked with sweat and dirt and tiny bits of grass confetti, so I went over to the Little Store for a cold drink, and when I walked in, Peggy Bradley was there. She was sitting in one of the chairs near the drink box, drinking a Pepsi-Cola and smoking a cigarette. Jack was standing by the drink box, and they were both laughing.

They both looked at me when I came in, and for a second, I felt like I had been watching a movie, and when it came time to change the reel, someone put a reel from another movie on. It wasn't a *bad* movie, this new reel. It was just abrupt. And it wasn't what I had gotten used to, watching the first reel. Only in this movie, the people on the screen realized something odd had happened, too. They somehow knew that the people watching had been thrust into the middle of a story and weren't sure what they had missed in the first reel, and the people on the screen weren't sure how to catch the audience up, so they just went right on, thinking, "They'll either figure it out or they won't."

"Hi, Mrs. Bradley," I'm sure I stammered. Then I just stood there; I didn't know what else to say.

Ladies didn't normally sit around in the

store. When they came in at all, they usually just got a loaf of bread or a quart of milk or whatever they came in for and paid for the purchase and left. I'd never seen one sit down and have a cold drink. Much less and smoke a cigarette. And visit. And laugh.

"You look like you've had a rough day, Slick," Preacher Jack observed. "You want a cold drink?" I suppose I stood there too long looking at Mrs. Bradley. "Cheerwine? Dr. Pepper?" Jack tried to nudge me off the awkward moment I seemed to be stuck on.

"Oh," I said, "yessir."

"Which one?" he asked.

"Which one?" I repeated, as if I hadn't a clue what he was talking about.

"Cheerwine or Dr. Pepper?" he asked again.

"Um...Cheerwine," I responded at last. Mrs. Bradley smiled at me.

Peggy Bradley was divorced. She used to come to the church sometimes. Not a lot, but every now and then. The other women at church used to talk about her. I didn't know what they said--I never actually overheard them--but when she would leave, they'd talk among themselves, and even I could tell they were talking about her. She was worth talking about, and she made it easy for them.

Peggy Bradley was what Gilbert called

stacked, and she wore these wide belts that cinched her waist and seemed to draw attention to the curves above and below. Today she wore gray pedal pushers, a black blouse with big white polka dots, and a wide, red patent leather belt that matched the red of her lipstick. Red right off a candy apple. The way she laughed made you want to say something funny, just to see her laugh again. Suddenly it struck me. Jeez--she must be Jack's girlfriend.

"Oh!" I said, and then winced when I realized I'd said it out loud.

"What is it?" Jack asked.

"Nothing," I said.

"You said, 'oh,'" Jack raised his eyebrows, questioningly.

"Yessir," I frowned, "but then I forgot what I was gonna say."

"Oh," it was Jack's turn to say it. "I hate it when that happens. With me, I just figure it was something I shouldn't've said in the first place." Jack held up four fingers.

"Huh?" I didn't get it.

"Maris," said Jack. "And four makes forty," he grinned. "It doesn't get much better than that." He took a deep breath and blew it out. We were all quiet for a few seconds. "Forty. And it's not even August yet."

"You ever seen 'em play?" I asked Jack, but

out of the corner of my eye I was looking at Mrs. Bradley.

"The Yanks?" he said, "Nope. Saw the Senators and the Red Sox once in an exhibition game."

"I'm gonna see 'em," I said, like I was going to tomorrow's game. "One day."

"Yeah, me, too," said Jack.

Mrs. Bradley laughed again. I smiled, because it was such a good laugh I just wanted to share a little bit of it. She dropped her cigarette in the Pepsi bottle and handed it to Jack as she got up from the chair.

"I'll see you tonight," she said to Jack.

"It may be eight," he replied.

"Then I'll see you tonight about eight," she smiled, and though she was half-turned away from me, I was pretty sure she winked. She crossed to the door, and just before she went out, she said, "It was nice to see you again, Slick." She said it real nice.

"Yes, ma'am," I said. And then she was out the door, but a little bit of her scent and a little bit of her laugh stayed behind. I heard her car start up, and while I was listening to it pull away, Jack touched my arm with the cold bottle of Cheerwine, and I jumped.

"Awful jumpy today," Jack noted and handed me the cold drink.

"Yessir," I said, "thank you," and I took the drink.

Jack took the empty Pepsi bottle with the now soggy cigarette butt and put it in the wooden crate and then went behind the counter and rang up 10¢ on the cash register, and when it cha-chinged open, he dropped in a dime.

"I've got money with me," I said.

"Good," Jack answered. "That was for Mrs. Bradley."

"Oh," I said for what seemed like the umpteenth time. I went and sat in the chair beside the one where Mrs. Bradley had been sitting. After a few seconds, I couldn't stand it any longer--"Is Mrs. Bradley your girlfriend or something?"

"Well," Jack began--then he paused, "she *is* a girl. And she is my *friend*. But I'm not sure we're at that point where I'd say she's my *girlfriend*. So I guess she must be 'or something.'"

He grinned, and I grinned back. She was something, all right. And we both knew it, even if we couldn't really say it.

# CHAPTER ELEVEN

Delmer Tukes' older brother Doyle was wild about a lot of things, but he was truly passionate about one thing--his car. A 1952 Ford--so black it had a purple undertone deep beneath the hand-rubbed shine. The chrome sparkled the way it must have sparkled in the imagination of the man who invented chrome. The tucked and rolled red leather bench seats had known precious few passengers, for it was a very short list of folks who were allowed to even touch "The Car."

Whenever Doyle rolled up to the gas pumps at Preacher Jack's, Preacher Jack simply walked out to the Hi-Test pump, re-set the pump, and stood, nozzle in hand, and waited for Doyle to pump his own gas. Doyle always got out, walked back and removed the gas cap, and then came and got the gas nozzle--careful not to allow any gasoline to drip or splash onto the finish of the jet black Ford. He always got three of the thick blue paper towels, and after he had finished pumping the gas, he carefully withdrew the nozzle, catching the nozzle in the cradle of paper towels so that no stray drops fell on the fender. It was more a feeding than a fueling.

Belief is a funny thing. Doyle believed the '52 Ford coupe with its deep shine and chromium sparkle was as much a monument to beauty as any

Grecian urn that ever sent Keats into ode mode, though Doyle certainly never knew of Keats or urns or odes. It didn't matter. Belief is what matters. Keats existed though Doyle never knew of him, just as beauty exists even though no one may exist who recognizes that which is beautiful. The beauty and majesty of the Grand Canyon or Victoria Falls would be no less beautiful or majestic just because no one had ever seen it.  Though I didn't fully understand it at the time, that was the gist of the first sermon I ever heard Preacher Jack deliver.

It was not what I expected, nor was it what I or anybody else in the congregation had been used to. There were no threats or admonitions, no dark warnings of hell-fire and eternal prices to be paid. On the way home that Sunday, my mother asked my father what he thought about the new preacher, and after he shook his head and grunted, she said that she thought it was thought provoking. My father grunted again and said he wasn't sure that church was the right place for thinking.

In the sermon, Preacher Jack went from this idea that beauty existed as a concept--independent of the existence of anything beautiful or anyone to acknowledge or appreciate the beauty--to the idea that the same may be said then for other concepts-- like love, like faith, like the very existence of God. Love exists though no one may be there to love or to be loved. We do not have to have faith--faith simply exists. Though we may not have faith, for example, others may have faith, may pray for us even though we don't know to or choose not to pray for ourselves. God exists on His own terms--He doesn't require our belief in him in order for Him to exist, anymore than the fact that someone halfway around the world may not know *we* exist or may choose even to disbelieve that we exist. And since God exists on His own terms, if He chooses to love us--even though we may not love Him back, or may even deny His very existence--there is nothing we can do about it. To deny beauty does not make it any less beautiful. To deny God does not make him any less God.

I listened and was surprised that I understood it even a little. And I didn't find thinking in church to be all that bad an idea. Others, I suspect, were more threatened by the ugly idea of the intellectualization of religion, though, than by threats of hell-fire and damnation. When it came to hell-fire and damnation, it was pretty easy to believe the preacher wasn't talking about them anyway. Belief is a funny thing.

Sometimes bad things happen even to the things we believe in most. Gilbert, with his entry into the teen years, had gained access to a whole new group of, if not actual friends, acquaintances.

Jimmy Barkley had just turned fifteen. Normally, a fifteen year old, of course, would have as little to do with a measly thirteen year old as a thirteen year old would have to do with a lowly kid like me, but all groups have their pecking orders. When you are the smallest, dorkiest fifteen year old--the runt of the teenage litter, so to speak--you have to turn elsewhere in order to get the recognition and respect that your full fifteen years so richly deserve. You might even have to turn to a thirteen-year-old. And so the Jimmy Barkley-Gilbert Campbell alliance was forged.

I knew the way things were supposed to go when you spent the night at Gilbert's. Being summer, you "camped out" in the loft in the Campbell garage. I had helped Gilbert floor the loft and haul the sleeping bags up there. I knew which board wasn't nailed down--the one you lifted up to get to the hiding place where the candles were kept. Not to mention Gilbert's stash of cigarettes--the ones he had swiped one or two at a time from his momma and dad. In the last year, a couple of magazines had also been added to the secret cache-- a *Photoplay* with black and white pictures of women wearing nothing but shadows, and most of a *Playboy* that Gilbert found in the trash behind Watson's Drug Store.

The idea was to stay awake 'til around 1

A.M., then sneak out. Gilbert would take along one or two of his cigarettes, and there you were--out and about in the middle of the night while the rest of the world slept. After about an hour of defying the laws of sleepdom, it was back to the loft. All-in-all, it was a real feat of pre-pubescent derring-do.

We didn't spend the night in the garage loft only in summer--just mostly. Special occasions during the other times of year might also warrant a loft sleep-over. Winter before last, the weatherman was calling for snow--a rarity and a treat in our parts--so Gilbert and I decided it would be an ideal night to sleep out. It was a Friday night, so if it did snow we wouldn't get a snow day off from school. We might as well get something extra out of the deal, so we figured an early start on the snow festivities would be a nice little bonus. Sure enough, it started to snow lightly around 11 o'clock that night. Then around midnight it picked up. We decided to go to the woods.

"Take the flashlights," Gilbert said, "but we won't turn 'em on unless we really have to."

Though it was gauzed by clouds, there was a full moon, and with the ambient illumination from the occasional streetlight or porch light playing off the snow, we could see well enough to make our way to the edge of the woods. Once we reached the woods, it was a whole new world--almost magical in the snow. We stood just inside the border of the trees and looked back at our tracks in the snow--nobody else's; just ours--like we were the only human beings in this strange white world.

Though we would never have said it out loud, we almost expected genuinely magical things to happen--as if the deer and the owls and the foxes might begin to talk on a night like this--as if you might overhear, if you were especially quiet and lucky, the enchanted animals speak of some secret that lay hidden in the woods--the location of buried treasure or an ancient Indian burial site. The silence wove itself around us like a fleece cocoon. We began to walk. Neither of us spoke as we walked. Words seemed too harsh an element to introduce into such softness. So we just walked--and stopped--and listened.

Eventually we made it to the creek, and we began to work our way along the creek bank back toward the Sugar Creek bridge and the road. The creek gurgled along beside us, but it was as if the watery murmur was to us alone--like the sound was for our ears only--like we absorbed every single soft sound wave before it could disturb the reverential silence of the surrounding woods. We stopped on the creek bank just shy of the bridge. The current picked up slightly as it approached the bridge, and the water raised its voice slightly as if it dreaded rushing into the black mouth formed by the creosote timber pilings. For a moment, we stood and watched the snow settle on the thick wooden railing along the top of the bridge, the scene dimly illuminated by a distant streetlight. Then, a gravely voice from beneath the bridge touched us almost physically,

"You lookin' for me?"

Of course we weren't. And neither of us paused for even an instant to consider if the voice was that of an enchanted fox or a benevolent owl with secrets to share. We scrambled up the snowy creek bank, snatching handholds of brush 'til we reached the road, and we ran. I don't know if Gilbert ever looked back, but I know I didn't. We ran until we reached the second streetlight, where there was a house relatively close, and we stopped to catch our frosty breaths. It hadn't even occurred to us to turn on the flashlights. With occasional glances over our shoulders, we hiked back to the garage, where we finally spoke.

"Who do you think it was?" I asked.

"I don't know," Gilbert replied, "a bum, maybe?"

"Maybe it was an escaped convict," I said.

"It wasn't Red-Eye Dick, I don't think," Gilbert added. "I didn't see any red eye glowing."

Red-Eye Dick was a legendary escaped

convict character who surfaced in late-night loft stories. Sometimes he was a serial murderer; sometimes he was the last of Quantrill's Raiders. Always he had lost his eye when someone thrust a red hot poker in it, and always he roamed the night looking for his eye...and any unfortunate victim who crossed paths with him. The last thing his victims ever saw was his red hot eye socket, still glowing with the fiery scar of the poker wound. He was certainly a likely candidate for midnight under-the-bridge voice, but, fortunately for us, as Gilbert pointed out, there had been no glowing red eye.

Of course, it could have been some *other* escaped convict, which presented yet another quandary: Should we tell someone? After all, if it *was* an escaped convict, we couldn't very well just leave him there to terrorize the neighborhood the way, in our minds, escaped convicts always did. On the other hand, how would we explain being out skulking in the woods in the middle of the night ourselves? Gilbert and I decided that our story would be that we awoke in the night and heard someone messing around outside the garage. We crept down, saw that it was obviously an escaped convict, and followed him to the bridge. That sounded entirely reasonable to us at that hour of the night. It was a good plan. Then it occurred to us that, if it was possible for us to have followed him to the bridge, it was just as possible for him to have followed us back to the garage--especially with our tracks in the otherwise unblemished snow leading directly back to us. We climbed down from the loft and jammed a rake in the mechanism that opened the garage door. Then Gilbert got his Boy Scout hatchet, and I armed myself with cans of spray paint and the cigarette lighter with which to create a makeshift flame-thrower, and we waited for daylight and the arrival of the morning paper. It was a very long night.

In the morning, the newspaper had no word of an escaped maniac. It did say that no more snow was expected, and that it appeared that schools would be open as usual on Monday morning.

Sometimes, in the late hours of staying in the loft, Gilbert and I debated who would win in a showdown between Matt Dillon and Paladin. It was an unlikely match-up, we knew. Basically, they were both "good guys." Gilbert seemed to attach a certain moral advantage to Matt Dillon because he was a genuine lawman--a U.S. marshal--and Paladin wore black, which in itself apparently removed him, at least in some degree, from the pure ranks of right and justice--he was, after all, a hired gun. We agreed that Paladin was probably the faster gun, but accuracy, not speed, and Marshal Dillon's absolute alignment with the forces of law and order afforded him the moral imperative and gave him the upper hand, according to Gilbert. I insisted that Paladin demonstrated not only superior quickness on the draw, but seemingly unerring marksmanship. Usually, the debate fell apart when Gilbert brought up the riddle of Paladin's first name. As much as I insisted that "wire" was merely a verb, denoting how one was to get in touch with Mr. Paladin--as in, by telegraph wire--Gilbert held to the notion that Wire was Paladin's first name. I would ask him if he had *ever* heard of anyone named Wire, and Gilbert would counter with "No, but I don't know of anyone else named Hopalong, either--which action-verbally, enough, was difficult to dispute. Ultimately, I held to the assertion that Paladin would never do anything to run him so afoul of the law as to bring the two of them into a showdown situation. Still--in the wee hours of nights in the garage loft--the subject came up. That's the way things were supposed to go when you spent the night in the loft. But now Jimmy Barkley had entered the equation.

It was the night following the day that the Department of Motor Vehicles made the mistake of issuing Jimmy Barkley a learner's permit. Jimmy Barkley needed a permit to drive like Eve needed a cider press.

The day before, Mr. Barkley had let Jimmy

drive him to the store for milk and Grape Nuts and cigarettes and then home again. Now nearly an entire day had passed and there had been no offer to let him drive, and it felt very, very unfair to Jimmy. He decided to spend the night at Gilbert's house, figuring the privilege of touching an actual learner's permit to drive ought to be worth at least two of Gilbert's pilfered L&M cigarettes.

It wasn't until after supper, as they sat outside on the porch, that Jimmy's eye fell upon the Campbell's green Plymouth stationwagon, and he decided that the honor of holding an actual official learner's permit to drive was worth far more than a cigarette--even one that offered "Less tar; More taste."

There were actually two cars in the Campbell's driveway--the Plymouth stationwagon and a 1950 DeSoto Custom 4-door sedan. The sedan wasn't an option--not even for a fifteen-year-old with a new learner's permit and an itchy gas-pedal foot. For one thing, there was the gear shift. So far, Jimmy Barkley's limited driving experience had only been behind the wheel of an automatic. For another thing, no one drove the DeSoto except Mr. Campbell. No one.

It was a gasoline-powered behemoth, a highway leviathan. It wouldn't fit into some parking spaces. For reasons know only to Mr. Campbell, he had painted the beast red. He hadn't *had* it painted, like at a body shop; he had painted it himself. With a brush. You didn't have to look too closely to still see the brush strokes. The scarlet road rocket was seventeen feet long and held itself nearly two feet off the ground. The only other creature that had any use for the crimson hulk was Tiger, the Campbell family's cat.

Tiger was something of an anomaly himself. He weighed in at nearly twenty pounds, and none of it was fat. That was his fighting weight. He also bore the scars that his affinity for fighting had earned him. Tiger had given up fighting cats years before--they simply provided him no challenge. He had moved on to dogs. Big dogs.

I had seen him operate twice, and it was a frightening thing to witness. It was a cold, calculated, and seemingly foolproof strategy, and Tiger worked it masterfully. He would lie on the metal sofa-glider on the Campbell's front porch and watch. The first canine victim that I saw was a boxer. The unsuspecting dog walked down the shoulder of the road in that near-swagger that boxers have, his jaw jutting forward, his pug nose in the air. About halfway past the Campbell's house, he stopped, then wandered a short distance into the Campbell's yard. He sniffed around a bit, perched on his front legs, lowered his rear-end, and began to do the dog-shit samba.

In mid-arabesque, Tiger interrupted the cur's concentration with one of those guttural yowls that sound like they'd be painful to produce. The boxer stopped what he was doing, stared in the direction of the porch, and lowered his gaze. Tiger eased down off the swinging settee, and changed his tune to an almost questioning meow. The dog took a couple of steps closer to get a better look. Tiger slunk to the edge of the porch, then out to the pyracantha bush at the corner of the steps. Once there, he took up a kind of taunting yow-yow-yow sound. Tiger glanced away from the dog only long enough to make a quick check that the DeSoto was precisely in place, then arched his back and hissed at the cocky boxer.

When the dog made his run at him, Tiger held his ground and hissed again until the charging, slavering beast was almost upon him; then he darted for the DeSoto and slipped neatly beneath it. Nimbly, he turned and continued to hiss and taunt the snapping canine, who then made the fatal mistake of belly-crawling his way under the car after what he thought was his prey. The DeSoto sat just high enough off the ground for Tiger to maneuver perfectly, but the dog was trapped on his belly beneath the chassis. It was an awful thing to listen to. But there was nothing you could do.

Later on, when Mr. Campbell called the animal control people to come and remove the dead dog from underneath his car, they said they figured what happened was that the cat blinded him first. Then, blind and wounded, the boxer found himself trapped with a wooly buzzsaw. Tiger never stuck around for the investigation. The animal control guy asked Mr. Campbell if he was sure this was the work of a domestic cat and not some kind of bobcat. Several months later, when Tiger did the same thing to a Chow, rather than get animal control involved again, Mr. Campbell just dragged the dog's body to the edge of the road and left it there, like it had been hit by a car or something.

When Jimmy Barkley--his new permit burning a hole in his pocket--looked around for opportunity with whitewalls, the DeSoto wasn't even an option. But the Plymouth--even if it *was* a stationwagon--would do nicely.

"I *can't*," Gilbert said, his eyes wide at the mere prospect of it.

"Why would they ever check to see if the extra keys were there or not?" Jimmy reached over and plucked a small cluster of the orange berries from a pyracantha bush.

"Shhhhh!" Gilbert looked toward the front door. "They'll *hear* you."

Jimmy bounced one of the berries off

Gilbert's head. "Whatta they got, super hearing?" He threw another. Gilbert tried to swat it away, but it, too, bounced off his head. "They'll never know. We wait 'til they're asleep; we put it in neutral, take off the parking brake, and let it coast out of the driveway. Then we start it and just go for a short drive, that's all."

"We *can't*, I'm telling you. What if they wake up and find it gone. They'll kill me. They'll send us both to reform school. They'll kill us and send our dead bodies to reform school."

"You've never been cruisin' at the South 21 Drive-In, have you?" Jimmy smirked.

"Well, no, but--"

"One of the car hops doesn't wear a bra and when it's late--like just before they close--she flashes the customers."

"No!" The mere chance of a glimpse of a real, live female breast had hooked Gilbert, and Jimmy knew it. For just a second, though, Gilbert almost threw the hook. "Wait a minute--how do you know?"

"I heard Darnel Johnson down at the Pure station tellin' one of the customers. Said she does it to get bigger tips. Says it works, too."

Darnel Johnson and his brother Jervis ran the Pure service station. Darnel had a '46 Mercury that he had hot-rodded and painted with flames along the fenders--all for the specific purpose of cruising places like the South 21 Drive-In Restaurant. If ever there was a voice of authority about what went on at the South 21, it would have to be Darnel. Visions of car-hop breast flesh had blinded Gilbert completely to the possibility of Jimmy putting words into Darnel's mouth.

"We could cruise in there just before closing time--just order a Coke or something, and--whammo!--" Jimmy pinched the front of his tee-shirt and twin-peaked each side out from his chest, as he positioned a pyracantha berry between thumb and forefinger of each hand in approximate nipple positions for a set of 38DDs--"titties to go!"

"What time do they close?" Gilbert was hooked, gills-deep.

"Two. We wait 'til about 1:30 to roll out of here; we ride down by the runway look-out--see who's still parkin' that late--those are the girls, ya know, you want to make a mental note of; then we cruise on into the South 21."

"And then right back home."

"Exactly. Nobody's any the wiser. Tomorrow morning, you just put the extra keys back in the drawer in the kitchen."

"I don't know...."

Jimmy pulled up the front of his shirt and quickly flashed Gilbert. "See anything *else* you like, boys?" Jimmy used his idea of a Marilyn Monroe voice. "It's almost closing time."

"All right," Gilbert caved in, "but if I end up in reform school, I'm taking your butt with me."

At 1:15 a.m., neither of them could wait any longer. They had smoked two cigarettes each already, and the house had been dark and quiet for a full thirty minutes. Getting the extra car keys had been easy--almost too easy, Gilbert thought, but Jimmy had said, "Hey, it's just one of those things that's meant to be, you know?"

Gilbert held out the keys to Jimmy and hesitated for just an instant--"You better know what you're doing, Jimmy. I mean it."

"Come on out and play with the grown-ups, dip-wad," Jimmy snatched the keys and headed for the driver's side of the Plymouth.

The next few minutes would remain forever etched in the memories of them both. They played it over and over in their heads until it carved out permanent little niches in that part of each of their brains where our scariest moments live and wait to leap back out at us with the slightest provocation.

The Campbell's driveway ran at a slight incline from the road to the house--or decline if you were headed in the other direction--but if you were pushing, it did require a bit of assistance for the first ten feet or so, until the slope and gravity took over.

Jimmy slipped the key into the ignition, but didn't turn it at all, out of fear that he might accidentally bump the starter. He disengaged the parking brake, and with the driver's side door open, Jimmy sat with his left foot out on the ground. Gilbert had the passenger side door open, and he pushed on the back part of the door frame, so that when the car began to roll he could hop into the passenger seat. Gilbert pushed with both hands; Jimmy, his back braced against the back of the seat, pushed backwards with his left foot, and the car began to ease backwards.

"Easy," Gilbert kept saying, "easy."

"Push," Jimmy kept replying, "push."

Suddenly, there was no need to push any more--the laws of physics took over. Gilbert leapt in and pulled the passenger door closed. Jimmy drew his left leg inside and pulled the driver's door closed. The car began to pick up speed.

At almost the exact instant, both boys saw the street light glint off of the purple-black fender of Doyle's 1952 Ford, parallel-parked in front of the Tukes' house, directly across the street from the Campbell's driveway. The driveway pointed like the barrel of a gun at the side of Doyle's precious Ford, and the two-ton sickly green Plymouth stationwagon rolled towards it like a giant bulky bullet caught in slow motion.

"Turn it!" Gilbert screamed, "turn it!"

Jimmy struggled with the steering wheel, "It won't turn!" he screamed back.

With the ignition key still firmly in the "Off" position, the steering wheel and the Plymouth were locked on target. It would be hours later before it even occurred to Gilbert to hiss at Jimmy, "Why didn't you hit the brake?"

"You kept yelling 'turn, turn!' How the hell could I think? Why didn't you tell me the wheel wouldn't turn?"

"You're the one with learner's permit! I thought you were supposed to know those kinds of things!"

There was just enough of an angle so that the point of the right corner of the rear bumper of the Plymouth came into the driver's door of the Ford like a battering ram. To have crumpled the side of the coupe so impressively, it was remarkable that the only hint of damage to the stationwagon was the slash of purple-black paint that adhered itself to the point of the bumper. But they didn't know that then.

The sickening sound of the thud and metallic crunch had no sooner stopped than Jimmy turned the ignition key, threw the Plymouth into "Drive," and floored the accelerator. Tires squealed; the stationwagon shot back up the incline; Jimmy stomped on the brake, and the car slid to a stop in the gravel driveway. He turned off the ignition, and the night was suddenly as silent as if it had never happened. Except, of course, that it had.

"Oh, my God," said Gilbert, "that was Doyle's car, wasn't it?"

Jimmy actually began to cry, "He's gonna kill us."

"He'll have to beat my father to it," said Gilbert.

The silence of the night caught back up with them both at the same time. They looked around. They looked at the Tukes' house, still dark and quiet. They looked at the Campbell's house, just as dark, just as quiet. They looked up and down the street, quiet and deserted. They looked at each other.

"Maybe they won't know," said Jimmy.

"Whaddaya mean, 'maybe they won't know'? You just smashed the side of Doyle's car in. You think maybe they won't *notice* that?!"

"Maybe they won't know it was us."

"Whaddaya mean 'us'? *You* were driving!"

"You stole the keys. You pushed. You think they're not gonna hang your ass, too?"

"Alright, alright. Let's go look at it."

"Wait, wait. Give 'em another minute. Make sure nobody called the cops."

They climbed over the seat, then over the back seat, and lay down in the back of the stationwagon. For several minutes neither of them spoke, then Jimmy said, "Your ol' man's got insurance, don't he?"

It was too much for Gilbert. Though a couple of inches shorter and probably twenty pounds lighter than Jimmy, it all suddenly blew up inside him: the whole night--the jiggly lure of car hop titties and the crashing disappointment of pubescent fantasy denied; the heady outlaw rush of stealing the car keys; the taste of pilfered cigarettes in the dead of night; the momentary thrill of the car rolling backwards and knowing that the adventure had begun; the helpless instant of impending impact; the sickening sounds of metal hurting metal; and now, the infuriating machinations of Jimmy trying to squirm out of the slimy mess he created. It was too much. Gilbert leapt directly onto Jimmy's chest, grabbed him by the front of his shirt, and began--as closely as he could envision the act-- to pound some sense into his partner-in-crime. It was, as it turned out, more a shaking than a pounding, and Jimmy recovered quickly. They struggled and strained and sweated and swore and snorted and scratched around in the confines of the stationwagon's rear cargo hold for a couple of minutes before they were both exhausted.

"Asshole," Gilbert hissed.

"Screw you," Jimmy gasped back.

But they both knew it was over. They both lay on their backs and caught their respective breaths and tried to untangle their respective thoughts until they heard a car pass by on the street. Gilbert rolled over onto this stomach, raised up and looked out the rear window. The corner streetlight offered just enough illumination for him to make out the awful mess that had once been the driver's door of Doyle's pride and joy. He thought for a second that he might be sick.

"Maybe we ought to go see how bad it is," Gilbert said.

"I gotta pee," Jimmy said back, "*you* see how bad it is."

They got out of the car, and Jimmy headed for the bushes at the corner of the house. Gilbert stood beside the stationwagon, and stared into the semi-darkness, trying to make the details of the damage come into focus, hoping it wasn't as bad as he feared it was. He couldn't bring himself to go in for a closer look. What if a car came by? What if someone came out of the house? What if the Tukes were all lurking there, peeking through the curtains, just waiting for the guilty party to return to the scene of the crime? He lit one of his L&Ms, then remembering that anyone watching from the house could see the glow of the cigarette, he ducked down behind the front of the stationwagon.

Jimmy returned and said, "Got one for me?" Gilbert didn't answer him--he just threw a cigarette at him. "Thanks," said Jimmy, "got a light?"

Gilbert threw the book of matches at him-- "duck down," he said.

"What for?" Jimmy asked.

"I think Doyle gets up about this time of morning to clean his sniper rifle," Gilbert snapped.

Jimmy squatted beside him and lit his cigarette. "What do you wanna do now?" he asked.

Gilbert just looked at him. "Just wait," he said, "we'll just wait and see."

And so they waited--for hours--with nothing to say to one another. Around five a.m., a light misty rain began to fall. They climbed into the back of the stationwagon and lay there in the damp quiet. It was what people would call "first light"--the sky had lightened, but not quite enough for the street lights to go out yet--when they heard the screen door slam across the street. The rain had stopped.

Gilbert and Jimmy slowly raised their heads until their eyes just cleared the tailgate of the stationwagon. It was not unlike the sight of an alligator breaking the surface of the water with only his eyes and his snout. The two peered through the misted back window. Doyle stood on the front

129

porch of the Tukes' house; he had a cup of coffee in one hand and a cigarette in the other. He seemed to gaze at the unblemished passenger side of the '52 Ford with a mixture of pride and satisfaction. It was the look of love.

If Gilbert or Jimmy either one breathed, you'd never have known it. Doyle finished his cigarette, set his coffee cup on the porch rail, and stepped back inside the front door of his house.

"He didn't notice!" Jimmy whispered.

"Of course he didn't notice, you dip-wad, he only saw--"

Doyle had reappeared, a chamois cloth in his hand. It was more than Doyle could endure, it seemed, to see the Ford's purple-black coat spotted with rainwater. He wiped the beads of rainwater away from the passenger side fenders and door and along the top of the roof with what could only be described as...tenderness. He walked behind the car and ran the chamois across the trunk as if drying the back of a lover who had just stepped out of a shower. And then he stepped into the street, and saw the driver's side, and...he screamed.

It wasn't a shout or a yell or even a holler. It was the terror-filled scream of women in horror movies, only a slight register lower. And it didn't stop. He screamed again. And again. He ran a short distance up the street, then reversed himself and ran a short distance the other way. His arms were outstretched. And still he screamed. It was what whoever coined the term "wall-eyed fit" must have had in mind. More than a conniption; well beyond a hissy.

"He's gone slap crazy," said Jimmy, sounding a little like he was going to cry again, "he's gonna kill both of us."

"He'll kill me first," said Gilbert. "He'll kill me just so he can get sent to the prison where they're gonna send you. So he can kill you *slow*."

Missrus Tukes and Delmer appeared on the front porch, their faces splashed with that wild alarm that comes from being awakened by screams. Missrus Tukes stayed on the porch and ran back and forth looking for whatever monster could evoke such behavior in her oldest son. Delmer ran to his brother, shouting, "What is it? What is it?" And all Doyle could think to do, apparently, was to grab his brother by the shoulders and begin to shake him violently, as if Delmer must have known who was responsible for this and he could somehow shake the truth out of him.

Doyle didn't really think that, of course, but in his crazed state of mind, he just needed to get his hands on *some*body, and Delmer was handy. Delmer, of course, had no idea what had happened, much less why his brother seemed to be attacking him, so all *he* could think to do, apparently, was to take a swing at Doyle. The blow caught Doyle precisely on his left ear, and with this new ingredient, pain, added to the mix, Doyle truly loosed his shaky hold on rationality and began to slap Delmer in the face. Together they tumbled to the wet grass, punching and grabbing and cussing and screaming.

Now--the early shrieks of the wall-eyed fit had awakened others besides Missrus Tukes and Delmer. The Stewarts, who lived next door to the Tukes, had called the police on more than one occasion about disturbances at the Tukes' house, so Mr. Stewart wasted no time in calling the police when Doyle's screams had jarred him awake this morning. The timing was such that the police car pulled up just as Doyle and Delmer hit the ground together.

Neither Doyle nor Delmer were strangers to the local police. Most of the officers already thought that Doyle and Delmer both were at least half crazy. When the two officers pulled the brothers apart and tried to sort out the source of the problem, *this* time, the exchange that followed did nothing to earn the brothers any sanity points with the two officers.

"She's just smashed!"

"--started shakin' me!"

"--she was fine last night!"

"--like some kinda crazy som'bitch!"

"--then he hits me in my ear--"

"--I thought the goddamn devil hisself had 'im!"

"--just tryin' to tell him 'bout the car and he hits me--"

"What the hell you talkin' 'bout? What car?"

"*My* car!"

"What about it?!"

"She's all smashed!"

"*Your* car?"

"That's what I was tryin' to tell you!"

"Who? When?"

"How the hell do I know?!"

"So you were fighting him," the first officer interrupted and pointed at Doyle, "because somebody *else* wrecked your car? And you were fighting him," he pointed his stick at Delmer, "because you thought somebody else was attacking him?"

"I...I guess. Why the hell aren't you out there catching whoever did this to my car?"

Once it was obvious that the fight was over, and since neither Doyle nor Delmer seemed to know why they were fighting in the first place, the first officer told them that he was not going to arrest them, but that he was going to take a report since they were responding to a complaint. Meanwhile, the second officer had begun to look at the damage to the '52 Ford.

Gilbert and Jimmy had remained hunkered down in the back of the stationwagon. Now, as the second police officer stood in the street and looked at the damage to the driver's door of Doyle's car, at the angle of impact, at the tire marks headed right toward the Campbell's driveway, and finally, at the green stationwagon parked at the top of the driveway, Gilbert and Jimmy flattened themselves against the bed of the stationwagon.

Jimmy began a soft, repetitive, chant, "Oh, shit. Oh, shit. Oh, shit ..."

The officer walked to the driveway entrance and stopped and looked again at the stationwagon.

Perhaps it was because the cops thought there was a kind of higher justice at work that saw to it that the troublesome Tukes family finally found themselves on the victim side of things. Maybe they really didn't make the connection between angle of impact, skid marks, and the old green stationwagon. Maybe it was time to get off work, and they just didn't want to be bothered. Whatever the reason, they told Doyle that some drunk had probably sideswiped his precious Ford, turned around in the driveway across the street, and taken off.

"Hit and run," they told him. "Too bad," they said, "that was a damn nice Ford, too."

As the officers got back into their patrol car and Doyle stood in the street looking at the smashed side of his beloved purple-black coupe, it began to rain again, a little harder than before.

## CHAPTER TWELVE

I was standing in the parking lot of the Little Store when Jack drove in. I had been playing a game I made up while I waited. I took one of the wooden Pepsi-Cola bottle crates and leaned it against a tree at the side of the store. It was a big old water oak that cast its shade over the spot where Jack parked his car.

The crate--designed to hold a case of Pepsis--was divided into twenty-four cubby-holes. Viewed long-ways--top to bottom, the way I had it leaned against the tree--there were four columns up and down and six rows across. Initially, I designated the four cubby-holes across the top as home run territory; the second row of four compartments would be outs--fly balls to the outfield, I reasoned; the third row down would be triples; the next row beneath that would be doubles; the four squares across the fifth row down would be ground outs; and the bottom row would be singles. Then, just to make it interesting, I decided that the two outside columns--six cubby-holes up and down each side-- would be foul balls, so that only the two inside columns--twelve compartments in all--would put the ball in play. It was Drink Crate Baseball!

I backed off ten paces and gathered up a handful of rocks, dubbed it Game One of a

Yankees-Dodgers World Series, and mentally flipped a coin, making the Yankees the home team. First up--the Dodgers. I tossed the first rock at the crate, and it clattered into the left outside compartment, fourth row down. Foul ball. That was close--almost a lead-off double. The next rock-- second row down, inside left column. Out! Ha! One away.

After each half inning, I emptied the rocks, resumed my spot on the imaginary pitcher's mound, and began my carefully calculated gravel pitches. It was the top of the fifth inning, the Yankees leading 6-2, when Jack pulled into the lot. I decided that the Yanks probably went on to win Game One.

"You're out and about mighty early this morning, Slick," Jack said, as he unfolded himself out of the green Bug.

"One, two, three," I said, "41, 42, forty...*three.*"

"I saw it," Jack rolled his eyes.

I followed him to the front door and held the screen door open while he unlocked the padlock and folded back the hasp.

"I believe that puts Mantle in the lead," I gloated.

"All right, all right," Jack said, "but there's a long way to go, you know." He went inside and behind the counter and set the padlock beside the cash register. I leaned against the counter.

"If he breaks the record, how much you reckon my Mantle baseball card'll be worth?" I asked.

He opened the cash register and took a quick tally. "Depends on how long you hold onto it, I suppose," he said. "I'll give you a dollar for it right now."

"I don't think so," I replied.

"Smart kid," he said. "I'll give you *two* dollars for a Maris."

"Don't have one," I said.

"Too bad," he grinned. "I'll give you a chocolate milk if you promise to hold onto the Mantle 'til you're my age."

"How old are you, anyway?" I asked.

"Older than rope," Jack said.

"That's an awful long time to keep a card," I observed.

"Okay," he said, "just hold onto it 'til you finish college then."

"What if I don't go to college?" I asked.

"Then you're stuck with it 'til you're older than rope."

"Deal," I said.

"Grab two chocolate milks," he said, "I'll join you."

Jack walked over to the drink box and slid

back the tops, peered inside and took a visual inventory. I fetched two pints of chocolate milk from the cooler. I set Jack's on the counter, shook mine, opened it, and took a long, smooth pull. Jack closed the drink boxes, went behind the counter, picked up his chocolate milk and shook it.

"So what'd you do interesting yesterday?" Jack asked. He opened his milk and drank.

"You mean besides watch Mantle destroy Twins' pitchers?"

"Yeah," he said, "besides that."

"Not much," I sighed. "Had to help my dad in the yard. How 'bout you?"

"Went on a picnic," Jack said.

"A picnic?!" I blurted, "where?"

"By the lake," he said, "at Freedom Park."

"By yourself?" I raised my eyebrows.

"No," he took another drink of chocolate milk, "not by myself. Peggy Bradley was there, too." It was all I could do to not chant a chorus of "Jaaaack's got a girrrrlfriend," but he must have heard it sing-songing in my head, anyway. "Don't even start, Slick," he said.

"I didn't say anything," I shrugged my shoulders, then I smooched the mouth of the milk carton before I took another swig. Jack looked at me. "What?!"

"One of these days," he said, "you'll

understand."

I didn't tell him I had a pretty good idea already. Sometimes when people think you're just a kid, it's better to just let them think that.

"It's kind of nice to have someone to hang around with," Jack said. As he turned the milk carton up to finish it off, a car pulled up to the gas pumps outside. Jack tossed the empty milk container into the trash can at the end of the counter. "Time to go to work, I guess." He started for the door.

"Jack," I said, "do you think I could borrow that Pepsi crate out on the side of the building for a while? I'll bring it back."

"Sure," he said, "help yourself, Slick."

Jack walked up to the car and spoke to the man behind the wheel--I didn't recognize him--then started to pump gas. I went over to the side of the store and picked up the drink crate from where it still rested against the water oak. As I headed across the parking lot towards home with the crate in one hand, I waved with the other. Jack waved back and kept on pumping.

# Chapter Thirteen

A new preacher showed up at church. Actually, the latest in a line of new preachers, but the others were what they called visiting preachers. We hadn't gone to church regularly since Preacher Jack's Sunday surprise. But, every couple of weeks, my mom would pick me up and off we'd go. My dad had really only gone before because of Momma, and with the separation and all, he wasn't feeling exactly blessed or especially worshipful, so it was only my mom and me. Momma had moved in with Granny, her mother.

Granny lived in the city, and she lived alone--at least during that particular period. Granny had already divorced one husband and outlived another, and we suspected she would find Number Three before it was all over. She owned another house, next door to the one she lived in--a huge, old, two-story, something-akin-to-colonial-style dwelling with a wrap-around porch downstairs and a veranda on the second level, and she had turned it into a boarding house for young women. Several events and circumstances had converged to bring Momma and Granny together under the same roof: the separation, of course; the fact that Granny was alone; and an incident back at the beginning of the summer. That incident became known as "The Day

We Started Locking the Doors."

We had no air conditioning--nobody did, really; at least nobody I knew--so once warm weather arrived, we opened the windows and doors in our house. As the temperature rose, we turned to an arsenal of progressively more vigorous fans, beginning with a couple of small oscillating electric fans, then moving on to a floor fan that resembled a large metal ottoman, and finally, the fan of last resort--the attic fan.

The attic fan was a serious mover of air. It drew a vortex of air through the house with such whoosh and roar that normal levels of conversation, loose pieces of paper, and small domestic birds, like canaries or parakeets, fell easily prey to its metal louvered mouth in the hallway ceiling. Day and night, the windows were open, the front and back doors were open, and only screens separated us from the summer nights. If we remembered, we would latch the screen doors at night with the hook-and-eye latches that otherwise clattered against the screen door frames with our every entrance and egress. "The Day We Started Locking the Doors" began with a phone call.

Momma was talking to Granny on the telephone. Granny had recently undergone some minor surgery. During her lifetime, Granny had, we were pretty darn sure, more surgery than any other woman on earth. Any place in the human body that stones could take up residence, they appeared in my grandmother, and they cried out to be removed. And so they were. There were organs, too, that simply couldn't stay--an appendix, a gall bladder, ovaries, and at times we wondered if she wasn't capable of organ regeneration--always faulty, always in need of re-removal.

We lost track of how many surgeries, and always she came through with flying colors. "The Day We Started Locking the Doors" began with a phone call to check on Granny after one of her surgeries, the exact nature of which has become lost in the excitement of all that followed.

While talking to my mother on the phone, Granny said to my mother, "Hold on. I just heard the front door open." Momma then heard my grandmother say something along the lines of, "What are you doing in my house? What do you want?"--a scream--"Get out! Help!"--the sounds of running and more screams--the sound of a screen door slamming--then silence. Since the phone line was still open, my mother ran to a neighbor's house and called the police. She then told me to get in the car, and we drove to my grandmother's house.

When we got there, we discovered that the police had already arrived and had found Granny next door at the boarding house where she was being attended to by two of the young ladies who lived there. She related a story of setting down the phone and walking into her hallway and discovering "a colored man" standing in her hallway. She said he "came after her," for reasons that were entirely unclear, but, everyone agreed, decidedly sinister. She had saved herself by running out her back door, jumping--post-surgical stitches and all--from her back porch, and running next door. The intruder was never caught, but the spectre of his entrance into Granny's house would haunt us from then on.

Later that same evening at home--it was the first time that I would hear my father use the "N" word to refer to a "colored" person. I had heard others use it, of course, but around our house it was considered a dirty word, right up there with the foulest of cuss words. So to hear my father utter the word--a man who was a master of the "near"-cuss word--dog-gone-it, dad-burn-it, karn-sarn-it, dog-bite-it, goll-durn-it, dag-nab-it, gosh-darn-it, dad-blame-it--just to name a few--was worth sitting up and taking notice of. And that night, before we went to bed, we closed the front and back doors...and locked them.

The windows remained open to feed the insatiable attic fan, but from that day on, when we went to bed at night, the doors were closed and locked. The whole thing also became part of the equation as to why Momma went to stay with Granny.

My father and I never really talked about the separation. The closest we came was a few weeks after my mom moved to my grandmother's. *Thunder Road* was playing at the drive-in. *Thunder Road* was my dad's favorite movie. I had seen it probably six times; I don't know how many times he had seen it--enough to sing along with the ballad as Robert Mitchum's 1950 Ford Coupe wound its way up Sorrowful Mountain behind the opening credits: "I can tell the story / I can tell it all / About the whippoorwill who ran illegal alcohol..." Whenever the movie came to one of the drive-in movies, we went to see it. The third weekend that my mother was away, it was showing at the Fox Drive-In. Since it was just the two of us, I got to sit in the front seat. It was the first time I'd seen a drive-in movie that wasn't framed by the front seat of a car.

About twenty minutes into the movie, I said, "Seems weird to be here without Momma."

"A lot of things seem weird without her, Slick." I waited a minute to see if he wanted to say anything else about it. "You want some popcorn?" he asked.

"Yessir," I answered.

He handed me two dollars. "You get 'em,"

he said. That was as close as we came to talking about it.

I wasn't thrilled with the fact that my mother was staying there at Granny's--not that I didn't love my grandmother; I did--I just wasn't all that fond of sleeping over at her house. I had my grandmother to thank for my only recurring nightmare. It centered on a character that I later in life decided was entirely invented by my grandmother: The Scratch Lizzie.

If you misbehaved, if you talked back, if you said bad words, if you didn't say your prayers--the code of offenses was voluminous, and only grandparents and parents were privy to the entire list, apparently--the Scratch Lizzie would come creeping in the dead of night and find you.

When the Scratch Lizzie came for you, she came with her long, terrible, razor-sharp claws, and she crept up on the sleeping miscreant child and startled him awake with her shrill, horrible cackle. When the child's eyes flew open--and that awful, shrieking laugh was guaranteed to make your eyes pop wide open--quick-as-a-flash--oh, horror of horrors!--the Scratch Lizzie scratched the kid's eyes out. Then, snatching up the naughty boy (or girl) in her cold, prickly grasp, she bore the little one away to her lair, where she kept him in a cage suspended from the ceiling until Halloween night, when she roasted all the children she had collected and fed them to her fiendish friends.

All things considered, it sounded a bit severe, as far as I was concerned. Yet something in the depths of my psyche was convinced that the Scratch Lizzie knew, not only the exact location of my grandmother's house, but the precise room in which I slept whenever I visited. I kind of hoped my mother--grown-up or not--was staying in one of the other rooms.

For years I had the same nightmare. I was at Freedom Park. It was nighttime. I sat on top of a hill looking down on a lighted softball field where my father was playing softball.

My father played fast-pitch softball for a team sponsored by the company he worked for. On Saturday nights during softball season, the league took over all three of the diamonds in the park, and every Saturday night my mother and I would sit in the bleachers and watch my dad and his teammates in their dark green and white uniforms and their steel spikes transform themselves into ballplayers-- not the grainy black-and-white big league mythical heroes who we had watched earlier in the day on the TV--but real, hitting, running, throwing, catching, in-living-color, right-there-in-front-of-you adult ballplayers. I loved it.

In the dream, though, I didn't sit in the

bleachers. I sat on this tall hill behind the bleachers, in the cool wet grass, in the penumbra of the ambient light from the ball field. In actuality, there *was* no hill overlooking the diamonds in Freedom Park, but in the dream, a steep, tall hill always rose above the field, and I always sat atop it--just at the edge of the darkness. I could see my father in the distance, out in right field, bent slightly forward, his hands on his knees, ready. My mother sat in the bleachers behind the backstop. She kept looking around, trying to figure out where I had wandered off to. I smiled because she couldn't see me behind her in the shadows, and I knew that later she would scold me for wandering off like that, but then she'd hug me.

And while I was sitting there smiling, I would feel a cold hand on my shoulder, and in an instant, the Scratch Lizzie would be sitting beside me. With the one hand, she dug her nails slightly into my shoulder. With her other hand, she first put her index finger to her cold blue lips, and said, "Shhhhhh." Then she placed her hand over my face, her claw-like nails resting on my forehead just above my eyebrows, ready at any moment to slash downward and take my eyes. I couldn't move. I couldn't speak. Between the hag's fingers, I could see my mother looking around for me, calling my name now. The pitcher fired an underhanded fastball to the plate; the batter swung and hit the ball; the ball lofted up, up, out toward right field. My father waited for it. The crowd began to scream and yell, drowning out my mother's voice as she called my name. And slowly the Scratch Lizzie pulled me back farther into the dark. Still sitting, I felt myself sliding backwards along the wet grass-- the bleachers, the softball diamond, and finally the lights of the field disappearing behind the crest of the hill. And then I'd wake up.

There was one thing that outweighed my fear of the Scratch Lizzie nightmare--I had for a few years gotten over any silly notion that there actually *was* such a clawed crone; so it was only the nightmare that seemed to come play inside my head whenever I spent the night there that I had to contend with now--but there was a treat that made even the chance of a nocturnal visit from the hag worthwhile: the boarding house that my grandmother ran next door. Ironically, I suspected that the attraction that the boarding house held was something that would surely run you afoul of the Scratch Lizzie--if she were real, and if ever she found out.

The old two-story house was home to ten young women. Most only stayed about a year, so every couple of months one of them would leave and another would take her place. The house was about six blocks from a hospital at which a nursing school operated. Many of the young women who boarded at my grandmother's house were nursing students. My grandmother's successive maladies and surgeries constantly tested their newly-acquired medical knowledge and nursing skills. It was a symbiosis that served my grandmother well. Other of "the girls," as my grandmother referred to them, had moved to the city to take jobs as secretaries and bank tellers and other occupations that the city offered and which simply were not available to them in the various small towns and rural communities from which they came. The accommodations were cozy and affordable and on the bus route, and so they came and stayed until they graduated or got a promotion or got married.

In the meantime, they roamed the house, secure in the knowledge that it was a "women only" zone, which meant they felt free to wander around in whatever stages of dress--or *un*dress--they wanted. Though I most often cursed my small stature and my baby-face, there were two circumstances in which my youthful appearance served me well. I continued to get into movie theaters on a child's ticket until well into my adolescence. And to the young women at the boarding house I was not really a male presence around whom they needed to guard their modesty and demeanor, but simply "a cute kid."

When I visited my grandmother, I found lots of small chores and other reasons to spend time at the girls' boarding house. There were three bathrooms--one downstairs and two upstairs--which the girls shared. They were treasure troves of femininity. It was there that I explored the mysteries of how women attended to the care and cosmetology of those hidden charms that had come to occupy so much of my early pubescent curiosity. In that divinely scented inner sanctum, I saw and touched my first set of falsies, figured out how bra clasps worked, and felt the cool, smooth caress of nylon and lace against my boyishly beardless cheek. When the weather turned warm, a visit to the boarding house for a boy of nearly twelve was the equivalent of stepping into a Victoria's Secret catalog today. And during those moments, it was "the Scratch Lizzie be damned." Though I still hoped she didn't know I thought that.

Gilbert claimed to have actually seen a grown woman completely naked before. Last year a professional wrestler named Billy Tomahawk moved to town. He only stayed about four months. I told Gilbert I didn't think Billy Tomahawk was the guy's real name, but Gilbert was convinced it was because the wrestler was married and had a son, and the son had been in Gilbert's class at school during

151

the months they lived there, and the son's name, according to Gilbert, was Billy Tomahawk, Jr. I still had my doubts, but I knew it was just another one of those arguments I'd never win with Gilbert.

The wrestler's wife--Billy Jr.'s step-mom-- was an alcoholic. Billy Jr. told Gilbert that his step-mom--Mrs. Tomahawk, I suppose--drank every afternoon until she passed out, and she always slept with no clothes on. Gilbert said Billy Jr. didn't seem to be ashamed of his step-mother's drinking or anything--in fact, he had come up with a way to capitalize on it. Billy Jr. told Gilbert that for 75¢ he would take Gilbert to his house and let him see his step-mother passed out naked.

Gilbert said they rode their bikes to the Tomahawk house after school one day. When they got there, Gilbert waited outside while Billy Jr. went inside to make sure that his step-mother was actually passed out like she usually was. Gilbert said that when Billy Jr. came back, he paid him the three quarters, and Billy Jr. told him to follow him and to be very quiet. Gilbert said they tiptoed to Billy Jr.'s step-mom's bedroom, and she was lying on the bed. They stood beside the bed, according to Gilbert, and Billy Jr. pulled the covers down, and, sure enough, she was completely naked. He said they stood there for about a minute looking at her-- Gilbert said you could see everything--then she kind of moved a little bit and Billy Jr. whispered that was enough and pulled the covers back up over his step-mom. Then they sneaked back outside.

Gilbert said it was "pretty neat," but that he thought he should have gotten to look longer for seventy-five cents. I told him I just thought it was creepy. Gilbert said, creepy or not, at least he had seen a grown woman naked, and I hadn't. I told him if I had to pay to see somebody's step-mother passed out naked, I'd just as soon wait, and besides, he was lucky that Billy Tomahawk, Sr. hadn't come home and scalped him or something. Gilbert said I was just jealous because the Tomahawks had moved away before I had a chance to see her. I wasn't jealous--it really was creepy, I thought--but Gilbert just didn't see it that way. Sometimes I wondered if there was something wrong with him.

## CHAPTER FOURTEEN

Like I said, there was a string of what they called visiting ministers who came to the church after Preacher Jack left. I think a couple probably were really visiting--preachers who had their own churches and who really and truly believed that by taking a Sunday off from their own flocks and coming to fill the pulpit of our floundering fold for a Sunday that they were doing a good thing--the "Christian thing" as folks were prone to say. The act was hardly diminished at all, I'm sure, by the fact that the visiting pastors got to re-cycle used sermons--got to share them with a whole new audience, so to speak. We were lucky to get them, everybody said, used sermons or not.

Some of the preachers were there as a kind of audition. Eventually, they found a new, permanent preacher to take over--Reverend McClain. He had a ruddy complexion and red hair, but, more importantly, as far as Rita Enslow and a few others were concerned, he was married and had two kids. What he lacked in spiritual fire and intellectual dazzle, he made up for in the trappings of stability. It would be nearly two years before the stable Reverend McClain's daughter, Denise, would turn up pregnant at age sixteen.

Additionally, the good pastor's son, Greg,

would be the one to introduce me to the perils of mixing Papst Blue Ribbon and Mannechevitz' blackberry wine. For those who may be keeping score at home, please make note that the two do not mix well. But...in the wake of the several visiting and well-intentioned clergy who had graced the church's pulpit during this rudderless period, the arrival of the seemingly stable McClain clan was an occasion for more than a little rejoicing.

If I'd've had my druthers, even at my tender age, I would've gladly traded my swimmy-headed introduction to beer and wine experimentation for fifteen minutes of learn-as-you-go time with the McClain family's sexually precocious daughter. It was, in fact, early rumors of successful ventures into the lacy, padded cups of Denise's brassiere that compelled me to accept an invitation to a party at the McClain's house at all. Greg, it seemed-- fighting the twin curses of a ravaged complexion and a PK label (Preacher's Kid)--did not hesitate to trade upon his sister's spreading reputation to lure potential friends into what must have been the truly weird world that PKs inhabited. Though I'm sure it would have killed me to know it then, it would be years before I actually captured one of the warm, jiggly bra dwellers in my young hand, and when I did it would not be one of Denise's. Getting permission to go to the party at the McClain house had been as simple as asking. After all, what safer socializing venue was there for kids and their pesky hormones than the preacher's house? Apparently, what folks failed to realize was that even in a preacher's house, when kids slip into a dimly lit basement, connections with upstairs piety are severed at an exponential rate with each descending step. If Disney had built an Adolescence Experimentation Land, it would've been built in a basement--though the rides with the longest lines would surely have looked like the back seats of Chevy Belairs, never mind how they got there in the basement.

"It was awful," I said to Preacher Jack. "Greg kept yelling at me to 'Clean it up! Clean it up!' but I couldn't. I knew I ought to, but I just couldn't. All I could do was lie there, and everything kept spinning around and around."

There are those who would say that blackberry wine and Papst Blue Ribbon beer don't mix. I can attest to the fact that they do, in fact, mix. The only problem is that they mix much as Drain-O and water mix. As I looked at Preacher Jack sitting behind the counter in the store eating Gerber's strained pears right out of the jar, I thought of the time Gilbert and I made Drain-O bombs.

Gilbert had gotten four baby food jars from somewhere and a can of Drain-O.

"We'll blow that sonuvabitch right out of the water," Gilbert said.

There was something--I only say "something" because we'd never actually seen what it was--that lived at the bottom of "the big pool" in the creek. The big pool--which is all we ever called it--like if we were planning to meet there, we'd say, "I'll meet you at the big pool"--was a place where the creek widened and got very deep. We figured it must've been twenty feet deep.

Supposedly Delmer Tukes had tied an empty paint can to the end of a rope and lowered it down 'til it touched bottom, then pulled it up and measured it. There was also "the little pool" that was a short distance upstream of "the big pool." Nobody but Delmer Tukes swam in the big pool. But then, Delmer was crazy; everybody knew that. The rest of us swam in the little pool.

Delmer had rigged a piece of cable--attached it to a big oak tree on the bank of the creek right beside the big pool--and he would swing on it, out over the water, like Tarzan, and drop...right in the middle of the big pool. Every now and then, he'd do that, and if anybody was watching, he'd suddenly holler, "Ahhh! Something's got me!" and he'd go under the water like something had dragged him under. Then he'd always come up and laugh. I guess he only did that if somebody was watching.

It's hard to tell with Delmer.

The little pool was plenty deep--probably nine or ten feet--and there were things living in it, too. Mostly carp, including some big ones. We'd caught one once that was nearly three feet long. Whatever it was that lived at the bottom of the big pool, we didn't figure it was a carp. Sooner or later carp come up, at least far enough for you to see them. Nobody had ever seen what this was at the bottom of the big pool.

I thought it was a catfish. I figured it was some monster catfish, maybe six feet long--too big to budge it if you hooked it. And we all had hooked it at one time or another. You'd feel it sort of move away--heavy and slow—and pop!--there'd go your line. Gilbert thought it was a giant snapping turtle-- six feet across.

"Take your whole foot off with one bite," he'd say, and--snap!--slap his hands together like jaws snapping shut.

For a while he tried to say it was an octopus that lived in an underground cave down there. I told him he was full of crap, but I had to look octopus up in the World Book Encyclopedia and show him that there was no such thing as an octopus that lived in fresh water before he'd believe me.

"Just like depth charges," Gilbert said as he set the baby food jars on the ground and unscrewed the lid off each one. The idea was to fill the jar about a third of the way with Drain-O, then pour in enough water to fill it about two-thirds full, then quickly screw the cap back on the jar and get rid of it before the pressure inside built up enough to make the jar explode. Gilbert opened the can of Drain-O and carefully poured the crystals into the jars until each one was a third full. "Go get some water," he said.

Gilbert had carried everything in this tin sand bucket with scenes of fishes and beach umbrellas brightly painted around the side in primary colors--the kind of bucket little kids play with at the beach or in a sand box. It was really all I could do to not make some kind of wisecrack about him and his "widdle sand bucky," but I thought better of it and went and scooped up a bucketful of creek water.

"Okay," he said, "now this is the tricky part. You wanna pour or screw on lids?"

I figured that if this was absolutely foolproof fun, Gilbert would've never even offered to let me screw on the lids, because whoever screwed on the lid then got to--or *had to*--get rid of the jar...before it blew up in your hand, I thought to myself. A brief, terrifying image of myself lying on the ground--blinded, my blown-off hand flopping around beside me, my face pierced with shards of

159

glass, the Drain-O hissing and bubbling as it ate away like acid at the bloody flesh of my face--flashed through my mind, and I said, "I'll pour."

"Wuss," Gilbert sneered. But I noticed he held the jar out at arm's length away from him, the jar lid at ready in his other hand, and his face turned away. I started to pour. "Don't fill it all the way up," he reminded me.

As carefully as I could, I poured in the creek water, and said, "Now!" Gilbert capped the jar and quickly threw it into the big pool. We dropped to the ground as if we expected an explosion to rock the entire creek bank. We waited. Nothing. "How long does it take?" I asked.

"Not long, I don't think," said Gilbert.

"Not *this* long, or not much *longer*?" I said.

"Shut up and wait," he snapped back. We lay on the ground and waited. After a few minutes, he said, "Something must've gone wrong."

"Like what?" I asked.

"I don't know," he said, "something."

"Maybe you didn't get the cap on tight enough," I offered.

"You wanna screw on the next one, dip-wad?" he answered. We waited another minute or so. "Let's do another one," Gilbert said as he got up.

I poured again. Gilbert twisted the cap on

and paused just long enough to see the mixture begin to bubble and cook. He tossed it into the middle of the big pool, and we crouched down. Again we waited. Nothing.

"Damn," Gilbert hissed. "Maybe it's the creek water. Maybe it's gotta be tap water."

"Water's water," I said.

"Yeah?" he shot back, "what're you, a water scientist or something?"

"I'm just tellin' you, water's water. It's a fact."

"Maybe you poured too much in," he said.

"I poured what you said," I replied. "You wanna pour the next one yourself?"

"Yeah," said Gilbert, "I'll pour and you cap it off."

That wasn't exactly what I'd meant. What I meant was, "Do you want to pour the water and screw on the lid and throw it? Do you want to do it all?" Instead, I picked up a jar and held it out. Gilbert picked up the bucket of water and poured. Quickly, I fumbled to get the cap on, twisted it 'til it caught and tightened. I felt the jar start to get hot in my hand, and I lobbed it into the creek. Several seconds later, a bubble about the size of a soccer ball rose to the surface and made a kind of "ploop" noise. We looked at each other. Was that it?

"Gimme that last one," Gilbert said. He set

the jar on the ground in front of him, picked up the bucket and poured in the water, screwed on the top, and sent it sailing into the creek while he made a whistling noise like a bomb falling. We waited. Nothing.

"What do you think?" I asked.

"I think you're some kind of a jinx, is what I think," Gilbert shook his head.

"Maybe whatever's down there swallowed 'em," I said. "Maybe it *likes* 'em."

"How 'bout I throw you in there and see if it likes you?" Gilbert said. He poured the rest of the water out of the bucket and started up the path, the bucket in his hand.

I trotted up behind him, and just as I passed him I said, "I like your widdle sand bucky," and ran.

The mixture of blackberry wine and beer actually turned out to be more explosive than the Drain-O bombs, and certainly more colorful against the white ceramic tile of the McClain's basement bathroom floor and walls. I figured I had done well to at least get in the vicinity of the toilet. The incident struck me permanently from Greg McClain's party invitation list.

Preacher Jack took another spoonful of strained pears, and said, "As much as it worries me that you drank in the first place, I hope it served to get the notion out of your system."

"It got *everything* out of my system," I said. I guess I expected him to laugh, but he didn't. "Not very funny, huh?" I asked.

The spoon clinked around the inside of the jar of pears. "No, it's not," he said. "But I'm fresh out of sermons."

The first time I saw him open a jar of baby food and start eating it, I thought it was one of the strangest things I'd ever seen. It was only my third or fourth visit to the Pump-n-Preach after it opened, and Preacher Jack and I hadn't really said much to each other up to that point beyond the rudiments of polite conversation and bread-and-milk commerce. Even though I didn't say anything--at least not out loud--Jack must've seen the expression on my face.

"Pears," he said. "Gerber's makes a mighty fine jar of pears."

"It's *baby* food," I turned up my nose and curled my upper lip.

"Does that make me a baby?" he asked.

"Well..." I wasn't sure what to say, how much I *could* say.

"If I ate dog food, would that make me a dog?" he added.

"You eat dog food?"

"No, of course not. But, I mean, if I did."

I just didn't know what to make of him.

Maybe they had been right--the ones I'd heard talking at church during the three weeks since he had walked out. Maybe he really *had* lost his mind. There were easily a dozen people that I'd heard say it aloud. They had no other explanation why a man of God--a minister, for heaven's sake!--would behave the way he'd behaved.

Somebody had suggested that maybe he had been drunk--that he was secretly an alcoholic, even--but nobody could remember ever seeing him drink, or having smelled alcohol on his breath. Somebody else asked where he would've gotten it without anybody knowing about it. Lott Felder, one of the deacons, and a man with a fondness for detective movies and TV shows and paperback books, offered to head up an investigation--to take a snapshot of Preacher Jack around to the liquor stores in and around town and see if any of the owners recognized him. But then his wife told him he was *not* Boston Blackie and never was *going* to be, so for him to just forget it, and Mr. Felder decided that, likely lunacy and possible alcoholism aside, Preacher Jack was smart enough that he would probably go somewhere way out of town anyway to buy his liquor and then just stockpile it somewhere like in his basement.

I wondered then--as I watched him feeding himself strained pears right out of the jar--if the folks at church knew about the baby food. I wondered if I should say something about it to somebody.

"Have you ever tried it?" Jack continued.

"No, sir," I said.

"Not even when you were a baby?" he looked surprised.

"Well, yessir, I guess I did when I was a baby," I answered.

"But you didn't like it?" he asked with an almost puzzled look on his face, like he was the one who should be confused by all this.

"I...uh...I don't remember," was all I could come up with.

"Oh," he said, "the way you looked--your nose all turned up and all--you looked like it was something that you remembered as tasting really bad."

"I don't remember what it tasted like at all," I told him.

"I see," he nodded and put another spoonful of the strained fruit into his mouth. "Want to try a jar?"

"I don't think so, sir. Thank you, anyway," I said, relieved for once to have my manners to hide behind.

"My treat," he held up another spoonful.

"I really just need to get on back home," I

said. "My momma'll be lookin' for this quart of milk."

"Suit yourself," he said, "but if you change you mind, remember--pears are the best."

"Yessir, I'll remember that," I nodded quickly and left.

I guess I watched him eat three or four jars during the course of what became my regular visits before I finally decided to try them. He went and got two jars out of the cooler where he kept several jars just for his own little dining treats. Though I sat over towards a corner of the room, so that I could hide the jar behind something if I had to, and kept an eye out just in case anyone like Gilbert or one of the other guys might come in and I'd have to try to explain what I was doing eating baby food, knowing all the time that there wasn't an explanation in the world that would save me, what I learned was the first of what would become many lessons--though lessons, I suspect, is not quite the right term. Things that somehow I knew I'd never really be able to share with the others--things that I would know and not know what to do with, at least not for a long time. It was a simple thing and a good thing to know, I suppose, but I just couldn't picture myself ever really working it into a conversation: "Gerber's, you know, makes a mighty fine jar of pears. And I prefer 'em chilled."

# CHAPTER FIFTEEN

"Miss Sarah," I asked, "is it dangerous where you live?"

"Dangerous?" she stopped ironing and set the iron upright on the end of the ironing board. "I don't reckon it's any dangerouser than anywhere else, honey. Why?"

"You ever notice when we drive you home--especially when my momma's driving--when we get close to your neighborhood, Momma always reaches over and makes sure the car doors are locked?"

"Yeah," she said, "sometimes I seen that."

"Is that 'cause it's so dangerous where you live?"

"I 'spect that's just 'cause she's heard stories, is all."

"What kind of stories?" I asked.

"Stories 'bout colored town," she said.

"What's it like in colored town?"

"'Bout like it is most places, I 'spect," she said.

"A colored man broke into my grandmother's house," I said.

"They's colored men and white men, too, do all kinda meanness, honey," she said, "but most folks don't mean nobody no harm."

"Then I shouldn't worry about you livin' in colored town?" I asked.

"Don't you worry yourself a minute about me," she said.

"What about Momma lockin' the doors?" I asked.

"A little door-lockin' never hurt nobody," she said. "You finished readin' about that football fella--Rockie Somethin'?"

"Rockne," I said, "Knute Rockne. No, ma'am, I still got a ways to go."

"Why don't you get your book and read me a little bit. It'd sure make this ironing go a lot easier," she said, as she picked up the iron and resumed pressing the sheet that was draped across the ironing board.

"Okay," I said, and I headed down the hall to get my book.

## CHAPTER SIXTEEN

I hated to see summer end. It wasn't that I hated school--I liked school, in fact, but with the return of school came the return of cold weather...sooner or later. And I hated cold weather. It meant bulky coats and hats and gloves, and still--riding your bike to school or trying to play outside--the cold found its way into your bones. If we were very lucky, there would be one, maybe two, snowfalls, and we could break out old sleds and flat pieces of cardboard and go sliding down the hill that led to Sugar Creek, but otherwise, it would just be the cold, and some days, that miserable 33 degree rain.

My idea of the way winter should work--I mean, if you had to have winter at all--was that the day that Christmas vacation began, it should turn cold. The next day it should begin to snow, and it should snow for two days. The snow should hang around through Christmas day--maybe a day or two afterwards. Then it should begin to warm up; the snow should melt; and by January 2nd, it should be back to warm weather. All in all, about a solid week of the best that winter had to offer. Everyone could plan for it. Everyone would look forward to it, like a well-planned ski vacation or something. I thought it was a wonderful plan, but Ol' Man Winter didn't seem to want to hear about it.

At least I wouldn't have to worry about safety patrol duties. Mrs. Jenkins had seen to that last year. Last school year had been my first and last year as a safety patrol officer. There was a certain attraction to the job's distinction--the wide white Sam Browne belt with its diagonal strap over the shoulder, and the badge, of course. There was the additional perk of a trip to Washington, DC at the end of the school year for all the safety patrol members--a week of no parents and impossibly overtaxed chaperones--a week of bus trips and new sights and hotel rooms and all the mischief an enterprising ten-year-old could get into.

My safety patrol duties meant I'd had to ride the bus most of the year, because I had to get off the bus at every stop and play crossing guard for the kids getting on or off the bus. Additionally, when the weather was cold, the kids who rode the bus home in the afternoons waited in the cafeteria until the bus arrived in the parking lot to load them up. I was to wait outside, and when the bus pulled up, I was to go inside and announce that the bus was there. During the last cold snap at the beginning of March, I had been waiting outside, watching for the bus, when I noticed the basement door slightly ajar.

I crept down the outside stairwell to investigate, opened the door, and called out to see if anyone was down there. Getting no response, I went inside and began to snoop around the basement. There was an old boiler that I found particularly interesting. And it was warm there. Then, in one of the corners I came across two magazines. I suppose the janitor had stashed them there--a *Playboy* and a nudist magazine. They were in a box labeled "Textbooks;" the top flaps of the box were already open. I looked around as if they had been planted there as a trap--as if as soon as I opened one of the magazines, someone would throw on all the lights, and the principal and my teacher and my parents and my entire class would leap out and catch me in mid-voyeurism. But, of course, they didn't. I went right for the nudist book, and--my God!--there was pubic hair! It was better than discovering pirate treasure. My heart pounded; my mouth went dry. I pored over the pictures of men and women lounging by a pool, sunbathing on a beach, sitting at a picnic table. I guess I lost track of time. Suddenly it occurred to me that I had been in the basement a very long time. As carefully as I could, I tore out two pages from the nudist magazine, folded them and slipped them inside my shirt.

Meanwhile, in the world upstairs, teachers and bus drivers and kids had gone about their fully clothed business. When the bus arrived, and no one announced its arrival, and no kids came out to board it, the bus driver waited and waited and eventually went inside to see what the problem was. The kids were loaded onto the bus--admittedly, late--and the bus went on its way--without me, of course--and when I finally wandered back upstairs, Mrs. Jenkins, the teacher who was in charge of the safety patrol was looking for me. And she was not pleased. She stripped me of my belt and badge right there on the spot. And, naturally, the Washington trip was not for those who, by way of their irresponsibility and dereliction of duty and sexual curiosity, had tarnished the safety patrol badge. It was a short and less than noble career. But the two pages of nudie pictures were mine to keep. All-in-all, I figured, not a bad consolation prize.

The highlight of the first day of school was Monnie Dietrich's new breasts. Over the summer, a few of the other girls apparently had been conscripted into the training bra brigade, but Monnie Dietrich had bloomed. And it was a bountiful blooming. These were no training bra recruits she was double-timing. This was full-fledged, card-carrying, high school cheerleader fantasy mammillation, and every boy in sixth grade was struck with a strange ocular affliction that skewed his vision to the corners of his eyes whenever Monnie was around. This was the year my grades would begin to falter, and teachers would make notes on my report cards to the effect that I seemed "distracted." I was not alone. It was a distraction epidemic. Monnie Dietrich was the Typhoid Mary of pre-pubescent male distraction.

After school, I stopped at the store.

"51 and 48," Jack said.

A package of two pink Snowball cupcakes caught my eye, and visions of Monnie Dietrich shimmered in my head. Jack's voice was lost in the roar of blood in my ears.

"Huh? ... I mean, sir?"

"51 and 48," he repeated.

It took a beat for his meaning to register.

"Oh," I said, "Mantle'll catch him this week."

"Detroit won't give 'em anything if they can help it," Jack pointed out.

"They've still got a month to go," I pointed out.

"How was the first day of school?"

"Great."

"Make any new friends?"

"A couple," I replied, and on their own, my eyes cut to their corners and stole a glance at the cupcakes.

"That's good," Jack followed my eyes to the pastry rack and looked a little puzzled.

"Think they'll make it?" I jumped back on

track, a little too quickly and innocently.

Now Jack was the one lost momentarily. "What? ... Oh! I don't know. It'll be close," he leaned on the counter. "They've both had slumps before. Never know what'll happen under that kind of pressure."

"I hope they do. One of 'em, at least," I said. "It'd really be neat if both of 'em did."

"Guess we'll just have to wait and see," Jack answered. "You come to get anything in particular?"

"No, sir. Just thought I'd stop by. Guess I better get on home."

"Homework, huh?"

"No, sir--not yet." I stole one last peek at the wicked pink Snowballs.

"Well--take advantage of it while you can," Jack leaned forward and looked again at the rack of honeybuns  and oatmeal crème cookies. Clearly, he did not see the attraction.

I thought of the two pages from the janitor's nudist magazine, stashed neatly in the bottom of a shoebox filled with baseball cards. "I think I will," I said.

## Chapter Seventeen

My grandmother kept "old sayings" tucked away like the good china. Then when the occasion arose, she would present them with something of a "ta da" flourish. Most of them I came to accept as gospel, pretty much, but some of them gave me trouble. "Don't be a stranger" always confused me because she always said it to someone she already knew. How could they *become* a stranger? "You've made your bed, now lie in it" was another. It always seemed to follow some wrong decision that someone had made, and it seemed to suggest that once a decision had been made, it was immutable, unchangeable, irrevocable--as if that was the nature of all decisions. And yet, couldn't you just *re*-make your bed if you didn't get it right the first time? These were not the kinds of observations that my grandmother viewed as refreshingly insightful. They usually prompted "A closed mouth catches no flies." That I understood perfectly.

Along the lines of "You've made your bed, now lie in it" was "Boy, he'd like to have that one back"--something that Red Barber would say when a pitcher would hang a curveball or try to run a high fastball past Mantle, and Mantle would send it rocketing out of the park. Somehow that phrasing rang truer for me. Maybe it was Barber's delivery.

Maybe it was the image of the pitcher turning and watching the irretrievable rise of the ball as it lofted over the fence.

The last game of the season was on Sunday, October 1$^{st}$. Jack and I had sort of planned to listen to it together at the store, but then Gilbert asked me if I wanted to spend the night over at his place on Saturday night and maybe go fishing on Sunday. I had to decide. Boy, I'd like to have that one back.

The last person we wanted to run into in the woods that Sunday was one of the Tukes, and yet as we approached the big pool at the creek, there was Delmer. Gilbert and I had spent the night before in his garage. Gilbert and I both avoided the fact that with his entry into junior high school, everything was likely to change. It was, in fact, changing already. Gilbert was feeling the pressure of some unwritten rule of growing up that said he must seek the company of fellow adolescents and shun the too, too dippy companionship of mere kids. We both knew it, but neither of us said anything. We didn't have to.

For most of us, entry into adulthood is less leap and plunge than gradual immersion. It is not like stepping off a cliff. It's more like our first swim in the ocean. We wade in--we feel its chill, the way it pulls the sand right out from under our feet--then we scamper back to the shore--venture forth again, a little deeper this time, until something strange and unseen brushes our leg--then retreat again.

The first month of junior high school had sent Gilbert scrambling back to boyhood several times. The weekends found him ambivalently back at my back door, seeing if I wanted to "kick around" a while.

At the end of September, Indian summer tugged at us to come share its last warm fling. So even as I felt him growing distant, when Gilbert invited me to come over and spend the night in the garage loft, I wanted those days back when we had been kids--both of us--even if it was just for a weekend. Even if it meant missing the ballgame on the radio at Jack's store. Besides, I told myself, Mantle was out of the race, and Maris had already tied the Babe, and his big bat had been quiet the last four games. It didn't look like he'd get number sixty-one, after all. At least that's what I told myself. And Jack would understand. I told myself that, too.

Gilbert and I slept late, and then we cooked eggs and bacon on the ol' buddy-burner. We had built the buddy-burner a couple of years earlier, following directions in a *Boy's Life* magazine. The burner element was an old tuna can--short and squat--made of heavy gauge tin. We had rolled a strip of corrugated cardboard, carefully cut to fit, height-wise, into the can without quite reaching the top edge. We had trimmed the length twice, so that, when rolled up, it just squeezed into the can, filling it completely. Looking at it from the top, it looked like a can of snugly packed honeycomb. Into the spaces that the corrugation created, we dripped candle wax--an entire red, emergency storm candle. When lit, the waxed corrugated fuel would burn for hours. The cooking element of the buddy-burner was a huge tin can like the ones that green beans or succotash came in for the school cafeteria. One end was completely open. The other end--what would be the top, the cooking surface--was punctuated along the sides, at regular intervals, just beneath the lid, with the triangular holes that only the sharp end of a church-key-type opener could inflict. To operate the appliance, we lit the burner, then placed the big can over the top of the burner. The holes along the side of the larger can simultaneously fed oxygen to the fire and acted as chimney, and the top of the can quickly became exactly hot enough to fry an egg or folded-to-fit strips of bacon. It could cook the perfect breakfast for a kid, even on the last Sunday of boyhood.

After breakfast we dug worms--red wigglers from out of the Campbell's flower garden, and I managed to capture two crickets. Gilbert didn't like to handle crickets. He'd never admit that, and he'd handle one if he had to, just to avoid looking like he was scared of them. And scared isn't even the right word--he just didn't like the way they felt in his hands--that scratchy thing they can do with their hind legs. I think--even though he knew better-- even though he knew they were harmless--that the feeling of them in his hand somehow tapped into the memory of an experience he'd had several years before--back when we were solidly both just kids.

Mr. Campbell--Gilbert's dad--had a "trick" that he used to do for us kids. He told us he could hypnotize bumblebees. To demonstrate, he would pick out a bumblebee and begin making this buzzing sound--bzzzZZZzzzZZZzzz--modulating the pitch and volume of the buzz in a fashion that supposedly mesmerized the bee. Then he would say to the bumblebee, "You...are...a...blue Caledonia butterfly," and he would catch the bee in his cupped hands and put his hands up to our ears so that we could hear the bee buzzing around inside his hands. And it wouldn't even sting him! Because, of course, the bee, in its hypnotized state, thought it was a butterfly. Afterwards, he would release the bee, telling it to "Wake up and be a bee again!" And away it would fly. It was actually a pretty impressive little trick--for an audience of kids, anyway. It wasn't until Gilbert tried the trick himself--and you can imagine what he got from the bee for his efforts--that we found out that the key to the trick was being able to identify *male* bumblebees--which have no stinger. The memory of the feel of a bug that clearly didn't want to be there in your hands had become imprinted on Gilbert, and even a harmless ol' cricket could conjure it back up.

Gilbert insisted on bringing along some of his lures, though they had never worked before. And even though I was pretty sure they were just the wrong kinds of lures for creek-fishing, I couldn't help but think that the problem lay at least partially in the fact that they gave off some kind of "Warning! Warning! Stolen merchandise!" aura to which fish were particularly attuned. We each had our rod and reel and tackle box, and we clattered like a caravan as we trooped through the woods toward the big pool that Sunday.

As the path opened into the clearing at the big pool, we saw Delmer. He was swinging on the cable that went out over the water. The swinging wasn't part of any swimming that Delmer was doing or planning to do--he wasn't even dressed for swimming--or in the case of Delmer, undressed. He had tied a bulky knot in the end of the cable, large enough to sit on, though not very comfortably, I imagined. He sat upon the knot, the cable stretched upward between his legs. He held onto the cable with one hand while he smoked a cigarette with the other hand, and he swung--back and forth--out over the creek--back over the brushy creek bank. When he saw us, there was no welcoming smile, no greeting. Even if there *had* been a greeting, Gilbert, I'm sure, would have missed it. He was already gone. Visions of Delmer and Doyle pummeling each other beside the wreckage of the '52 Ford flashed before Gilbert, and he turned on his guilty, sneaker-clad heels and ran. Though I was not sure at that point *why* such a sudden and speedy retreat was in order, I wasn't about to hang around and see if Delmer could fill in the blanks for me, so I, too, turned and took off after Gilbert. I did hear Delmer shout something as I ran, but I couldn't make out what it was. I was pretty sure it wasn't, "Come back, guys--let's be friends!"

Gilbert didn't slow down 'til he made it back to the road. When I caught up with him, he was huffing and puffing, but he managed to gasp, "Is he comin'?" When I didn't answer quickly enough, he asked again, more urgently, "Is he comin'?!"

"No," I said, "he's just swingin'." Gilbert bent at the waist and caught his breath. "I take it we're not going fishing," I said.

"Not unless you want Delmer Tukes to use you for bait," Gilbert answered.

"We didn't do anything to him," I said, more than a little annoyed that our fishing trip was spoiled.

"Maybe *you* didn't," Gilbert replied, still keeping an eye on the path into the woods.

"Why? What'd *you* do to Delmer?" My curiosity was more than a little piqued.

"Nothin'," said Gilbert. "Let's get outa here." And he picked up his stuff and started up the road.

I realized that now--whatever Gilbert had done that gave him reason to flee at the sight of Delmer Tukes--I was guilty by association in the mind of Delmer. I supposed even Delmer had a mind. Of some sort. I trotted to catch up with Gilbert.

"So're you gonna tell me what you did?"

"Not here."

"Where?"

"I'll tell you later. Let's take this stuff home," Gilbert said.

"I'll buy you a Doctor Pepper," I offered, thinking, I suppose, that the sweet elixir of cola and fruit flavors would loosen his tongue.

"Where?" Gilbert asked.

"Let's go by Preacher Jack's store," I said.

"Think he'll buy the worms off us?" Gilbert held up the cup of red wigglers.

182

Jack rarely carried bait at the store--
sometimes a few cardboard containers of night
crawlers on holiday weekends, like the 4th of July--
but I was pretty sure he would swap us a candy bar
for the handful of worms from the Campbell's
flower bed, even though he would probably just
take them out back and dump them in the woods at
the back of the store after we were gone. Jack was
just like that.

"We can probably make some kind of deal,"
I told Gilbert. It was enough.

"All right," he said, "let's go."

# CHAPTER EIGHTEEN

As we crunched across the gravel of the Little Store's lot, Preacher Jack was out front gassing up a green Ford pickup. Mr. Edmundston sat behind the wheel of the truck and looked at himself in the truck's rear view mirror. He moved his chin up and to the right, stretching the skin taut across his jawline and up along his neck. He ran his hand over his skin, feeling its tone, lowered his chin and slapped up at his doubling chin with the backside of his fingers. Mr. Edmundston was the phys ed teacher at Gilbert's junior high school. Mr. Edmundston kept a constant check in whatever mirror happened to be handy on the effects of aging and other things on what must have once been a fairly athletic body--otherwise, how could he have become a coach and a P.E. teacher?--but a body which now suggested encounters more with the cafeteria line than the scrimmage line. As we walked up, he handed Jack three dollars for the gas, looked at us, nodded, and said, "Gentlemen," by way of both greeting and leaving. Mr. Edmundston addressed all of his students--the boys, at least--as "Gentlemen," with an almost drill instructor edge to his voice. He started the engine, dropped the pickup in gear, and rolled away, across and out of the lot. Gilbert and I waved away the dust cloud with our hands.

Jack looked at us--fishing poles in our hands--and asked, "Coming or going?" as he started for the store.

"Huh?" I said, then caught his meaning. "Oh--coming, I guess."

"Catch anything?" Jack opened the screen door and held it for us.

"No, sir," I answered.

"Somebody had our spot," Gilbert added.

"Oh," said Jack, "too bad."

As we crossed the threshold, the voice of Phil Rizzuto greeted us from the radio. *At the end of three and a half, it's Boston nothing and the Yankees nothing.*

"Wanna buy some worms?" Gilbert held up the cup.

"They'd have to be especially tasty worms," Jack said. "Have you tried 'em?"

*Tony Kubek to lead off for the Yankees. Tony's single to center field in the first inning is the Yankees' lone hit off Tracy Stallard, the big right-hander,* Rizzuto chimed in. *And on deck, Roger Maris.*

"You mean *ate* any?" Gilbert turned up one corner of his upper lip and scrunched his face.

"I suppose that's one way," Jack nodded seriously, then he grinned, "or you could have the fish try 'em is another way."

*The wind-up, the pitch to Kubek. It's a swing and a miss--strike one.*

"We didn't get a chance," I said.

"So they're freshly dug worms?" Jack reached out for them. Gilbert handed him the cup. Jack reached in, moved the dirt around a little with his fingers, and pulled out a red wiggler. "This morning?" he asked.

*Stallard comes back with a curve.*

"Yessir," I said, taking over the transaction.

*Swung on and missed--strike two. Nothing and two to Tony. They were both low, breaking curve balls, down and in, below the knees.*

"They *look* tasty enough," Jack said, raising the squirming bait right in front of his face. For just a second, you had to wonder if he was going to actually take a bite to test the earthworm's flavor and freshness.

*Now the two strike pitch. Another curve-- low, inside. One ball, two strikes. Right now, let's pause for station identification.*

After a sufficiently thorough examination of the worm from all angles, Jack dropped it back into the cup and flicked some dirt over it with his finger.

*This is WBT in Charlotte. The time: 18 minutes before 3 p.m.*

"Tell you what I'll do," he said, "I'd be

willing to go as high as two Dr. Peppers and a Zagnut for the whole lot."

*A one ball, two strike count on Kubek, leading off here in the bottom of the fourth. Scoreless ballgame.*

A Zagnut was very splitable. It seemed like a more than generous offer to me.

*Curve is low, and the count is even at two and two.*

"Deal," I said, and I looked at Gilbert. Gilbert nodded his agreement.

"Think I'll put these babies in the cooler in the back," Jack headed for the back part of the store. "You guys grab yourselves a drink."

*The two-two pitch. Strike three call. The curve ball caught the outside part of the plate. Second strikeout for Stallard, and here comes Roger Maris.*

Gilbert and I opened the drink box and fished out two cold ones. Jack came back and walked over to the candy counter. He tossed me a Zagnut.

"You do the divvying up duties," he said.

*Last time up, Roger hit one deep to left field. It crossed everybody up, including Yastrzemski, who made a fine catch. He was so surprised, Maris hitting the ball in left.*

I opened the wrapper and snapped the candy

bar in two. I eyed the two pieces. It was an almost perfect split. One of the halves may have been a smidgen bigger than the other, so just to avoid any complaints I handed it to Gilbert. As Jack went behind the counter and rang up the three dollar gasoline purchase, Gilbert and I hopped up onto the drink box and began to munch our treats.

*We only got a handful of people sitting out in left field, but in right field, man, it is mobbed out there. And they're standing up, waiting to see if Maris is going to hit number 61.*

Gilbert had finished his half of the Zagnut and was working on his Dr. Pepper. Gilbert always was a guzzler. I was usually more of a sipper.

*Here's the wind-up, the pitch to Roger. Way outside--ball one. And the fans are starting to boo.*

Just then the door opened, and Delmer Tukes clumped inside. He stood there a moment and sneered at us.

*Maris only has--including this time--three times at bat, and unless the Yankees get a rally, that's all he'll have to try to get number 61 on the year.*

"Git down," Delmer snorted at us and started toward the drink box.

*The wind-up, the pitch--low, ball two. That one was in the dirt. And the boos get louder.*

I assumed he wanted a cold drink, and I

hopped down and stepped out of his way. I'm not sure what Gilbert assumed.

*Two balls, no strikes on Roger Maris.*

I saw Gilbert pull up his pants leg and reach into his boot. I felt the blood rush from my face, as I realized what he was reaching for. My throat closed up--I couldn't say anything.

*Here's the wind-up.*

Delmer, of course, didn't have a clue, as he reached out to push Gilbert out of the way. Jack straightened up and started to say something, but before he could speak, we all saw the .25 in Gilbert's hand. Delmer snatched at the gun.

*Fast ball--hit deep to right, this could be it! Way back there!*

I couldn't tell whose hand it was in when it went off--a sharp, irrevocable pop--but somewhere in the process, Delmer grabbed it, or Gilbert let it go.

*Holy Cow, it's number sixty-one for Maris!*

For just an instant, it was in Delmer's hand, as we all turned towards Jack, who had fallen back against the wall, then collapsed to the floor out of sight behind the counter.

*Look at 'em fight for that ball out there! Holy Cow! What a battle.*

Delmer dropped the gun. I tried to yell, but nothing would come out.

*Another standing ovation for Roger Maris.*
*Sixty-one home runs, and they're still fighting for*
*that ball out there. People are climbing over each*
*other's backs.*

Gilbert just sat there atop the drink box, shaking.

*And they want Maris to come out and take*
*another bow. He does.*

Then everything seemed to freeze. There was no sound. It was suddenly as soft and surreal as that snowy night in the woods, as if someone had wrapped the moment in cotton.

The world beyond that moment came back in stages--in a series of waves that washed over me. First, movement returned--and for a second or two seemed to move in fast-forward, as if to make up for the frozen moment. Then, there was sound-- though it all seemed too loud and tinged with echo.

*One of the greatest sights I've ever seen*
*here in Yankee Stadium.*

Delmer burst forward toward the door. Gilbert drew himself into a ball atop the drink box, his mouth open, but silent, and his head shaking. Delmer hit the screen door running. There was the sound of a car horn outside. I heard myself calling out, "Jack!" I ran around the end of the counter and grabbed Jack by the arm. His eyes were closed, but his left eye was swollen, and a stream of blood ran from beneath the eyelid and down his cheek, onto the left side of his chest, onto his left arm, onto the floor.

*And they're still applauding, and everybody's looking out in right field, because that baseball is worth at least six thousand dollars and a round-trip ticket to the Seattle World's Fair.*

I kept calling him--"Jack! Jack!" even though I knew he wasn't coming back. The screen door opened again, and a man I'd never seen before stepped from the bright unsuspecting world of the-way-things-had-always-been into the hazy land of everything-just-changed.

*Yogi Berra's up, but nobody knows it.*

The man was on his way home to Georgia from a visit to his wife's family in Norfolk, Virginia. He had only stopped to get gas. His wife and their two daughters were in the car, parked at the pumps. "Help. Please," I said to the stranger silhouetted in the doorway, "he's shot right in the eye." I guess that's what I said. Later on, that's what the stranger would tell them I said.

*All eyes are out toward right field. They were on the Yankees' dugout, but they're out on that little spot in right field.*

191

# CHAPTER NINETEEN

Jack said one time while we were just sitting around talking that every conversation was a kind of miracle. He said that with time stretching forever frontwards and backwards, and with space stretching forever in all directions, the fact that two creatures met at exactly the same intersection of time and space in the midst of all that infinity was remarkable in itself, but when you factor in that those two creatures could say or do something by which they both acknowledged and understood each other and the fact that there they were--standing at that same intersection on the map of eternity--and that they would both leave that spot, but take that moment with them forever--was nothing short of a miracle. I have sometimes wondered how many times that man from Georgia or his wife or their two daughters told the story of pulling into this little store just to get some gas and discovering that they had wandered smack into the middle of a man getting shot dead. I wondered *how* they told the story--which details stuck in their memories, whether they made up stuff to fill in the blanks. I wondered about the people they told the story *to*. Did they believe it? Were they shocked? Sympathetic? Did the man's buddies laugh the way some people do and say things like, "Damn! You sure got a knack for steppin' in shit, doncha?" Did any of them remember Jack's name? Or was he reduced to "the guy who got shot"? I wondered if, when the two little girls grew up and got married, one of them had a son and she named him Jack, did that *mean* anything or was that just one of those weird things that happens?

The stranger told me to go outside. I said, "Gilbert..." and pointed to him still on top of the drink box, and the stranger looked and saw Gilbert and said, "Outside, boys. Both of you boys get outside." He must've seen the gun on the floor, too, and he probably wasn't sure whether Gilbert or I or Delmer, whom he had seen run out also, were involved or how, because he told us to go over by the VW and wait. Over by Jack's car--not his car, where his wife and their two daughters sat with growing apprehension and curiosity about what was going on. Apparently, the stranger used Jack's telephone then to call the police. The deputies and the sheriff himself got there pretty quick, I suppose--my sense of time was all out of kilter.

Gilbert didn't go back to junior high school on Monday like he was supposed to. He went away to a school that the state juvenile authorities ran. He stayed there for a few years, and when he got out, he came home and tried to go to high school for a while, but it just didn't work out. He went in the Navy, though, and that seemed to suit him just fine, because he stayed in most of his life. Delmer never did stay out of jail very long for the rest of his life. And me--well, I'm okay. I missed more days of school than usual that year. Momma moved back home.

One Monday after school, a few weeks later, I got on my bike and rode to the small cemetery where Jack was buried. I hadn't been there since the funeral. There's a little store and gas station--a lot newer and fancier than Jack's--just down the road from the cemetery. I stopped at the store and bought a Dr. Pepper and then pedaled on down to the entrance to the graveyard. I held the Dr. Pepper with my right thumb and forefinger wrapped around the neck of the bottle, my other three fingers gripping the handlebar. The bottle hung down and rocked as I pedaled, the metal teeth on the underside of the bottle cap digging into the web of skin between my thumb and finger. But I didn't really mind the dull pain. I got off and pushed my bike along the driveway that curved past the rows of markers and headstones. Toward the back, in the corner, is where they had buried Jack. He had a headstone--nothing fancy--just his name and his birthday and the date of that day in the store. I didn't stay long. I took a newspaper clipping from the October second's morning paper out of my shirt pocket and unfolded it. There was an article and a big headline and a picture of Roger Maris in mid-swing. I placed it on top of the headstone and smoothed it out and set the unopened Dr. Pepper bottle on it to hold it down. I sucked on the red teeth marks where the bottle cap had bitten into my hand. There was a little bit of a breeze, and one end of the headline flapped around a little, so I looked around and found a rock and set it on top of that corner of the piece of paper. I remembered seeing a movie one time that showed Jewish people setting rocks on top of somebody's headstone, and I wondered what it meant. I thought, "I bet Jack'd know why they did that." I couldn't think of anyone else at the moment who might know.

"Maris made it, Jack," I said. "Just in case you missed it."

I picked up my bike and walked it back to the entrance to the cemetery. I turned and looked back at the headstone, then swung my leg over the crossbar, felt the pedal settle solidly into the notch where heel meets sole, raised up, pushed off, and headed down the road. The wind was cooler, but not unkind. For the moment, it just felt nice to ride.

The weeds from the old Sutton place eventually took over the Little Store, and finally somebody tore it down and put up a MacDonald's. But I remember what *was* there.

I remember. And I still have the Mantle card.

## THE END